Breach

By

Marie Dunn

D1715861

Also By Marie Dunn

A Thousand Awkward Moments

Bradford Place

&

Ladies of Lorton Landing

Acknowledgements

Thank you to my constant sounding board and husband Dave, who humors me by living in my alternative world of hypothetical plot lines.

Thank you to my proofreaders Anna and Judy and to my writing group especially Kristy and Sue for reading and rereading changes and challenging my story and characters.

Thank you to my editor, Faith Freeman, for her expertise and final touches on my story.

Thank you to my cover artist, Dar Albert, for picturing my words.

And most of all, thank you to my readers. I appreciate your kind words and encouraging emails.

Table of Contents

Chapter 1
Deceived

Monday, May 9th, 4:28 a.m.

Lana watched the clock tick off the final minutes before the alarm sounded and marked the start of her last day in America...or possibly on earth.

Quiet blanketed the apartment like the calm before a storm. A wave of regret washed over her as she reached over and tapped the button to stop what had already been set in motion—4:29 a.m. It was too late to second-guess her day; chaos was already in place, and silencing the alarm wouldn't halt the plan.

She closed her eyes to push back the creeping sadness and snuggled closer to Cal, prolonging the last moments she would ever spend with him. It was her twenty-eighth day in America, and she had never dared to dream a life like this existed. She listened to his rhythmic snores and pretended this was her life.

When she first heard her name called along with the other Syrian fighters chosen to bring jihad to America, her heart swelled with great pride. She was elated and determined to prove she was worthy of the call. It was like winning the ISIL lottery. She would be one of the first female ISIL fighters to be sent to America. She had learned English by listening to American music and watching countless American movies when she was living in orphanages and foster homes.

The last foster home had finally broken her. She was barely thirteen when she heard her new foster father open the bedroom door and whisper her name. Something about his tone set off warning signals, and she pretended to be asleep. Her skin crawled when his hands moved over her body, squeezing and pinching and prodding while she pretended to be having a nightmare. And then the tearing pain. She tried to scream. But he just continued with his hand covering her mouth to smother the sound.

The next morning, the minaret loudspeakers blared outside her window from hundreds of mosques, calling Muslims to their ritual duty of morning prayer. No one said a word. She was expected to pray and do her chores as if nothing had happened.

A few nights later, her heart pounded when she heard him open the door again, but she was no longer an innocent thirteen-year-old. She gripped the kitchen knife she'd stashed under her pillow. Hate, fear, and panic fueled her adrenaline when he climbed into her bed. When his sweaty hand covered her mouth, she struggled for breath. The intensity of the fight gave her the strength to drive the knife into his back and shove him to the floor. She'd felt empowered for the first and only time in her young life when she grabbed the bag she had packed and ran from the house to the streets. She had been running and fighting ever since that night.

Cal spooned closely behind Lana and threw his muscled arm and leg over her. He rubbed his thick, scratchy stubble against her shoulder and kissed her neck. "Stay in bed with me. You don't need to run this morning; you already have the perfect body."

Lana pushed back her long hair and embraced Cal's arm, snuggling it between her breasts, luxuriating in the security of his warm bed.

"How can you say that? I have gained fifteen pounds since I've been here."

Cal caressed her soft flesh, nuzzling soft kisses against her neck. "I love every inch of you."

She grudgingly remembered the names on the list. *Today was the day.* "I have to run early. I have an interview this morning."

"You don't need a job; I'll take care of you."

Lies slid off her tongue like silk. "I have to get job, or my visa will be pulled. Too many people helped me to get here, and are depending on me." She was as good as dead, and so was Cal, if she allowed herself to be sidetracked by her feelings now.

Cal planted a kiss on her shoulder. "My mother wants to meet you. She's been bugging me for the past week. Why don't we drive over to Annapolis today after my finals? We could have lunch, and you could meet my parents."

A tiny place in her heart longed for a relationship with a real mother. She had forced herself to bury the last childhood memory of her own mother. The deafening scream of the bomb blast that took her still echoed in Lana's ears. Her mother had gripped her hand and hadn't let go, even in death. Lana was haunted throughout her childhood by the smells of burning flesh and the stickiness of her mother's blood covering their entwined fingers until Lana was finally forced to pull her hand free.

She had set her scruffy-looking stuffed bunny on the ground so she could pry her mother's hand away. Someone pulled on her coat to run. She was yanked away kicking and screaming, "Momma, Momma," until she was too hoarse to whisper and too far away to run back. Later, she realized she had left her only possession in the world behind. She kept rubbing the pocket inside her coat between her little fingers, pretending it was her bunny's ear. She was all cried out. The only solace was that her beloved bunny was with her mother. They would have each other.

No one had cared about *her* mother when they bombed her and left her in the street like an animal. Bitterness filled the emptiness created by her longing.

Cal nudged her with another kiss. "Well, what do you think? I'll even sweeten the offer and make you pancakes."

She couldn't get used to having a man catering to her. In Syria, she was completely disposable. To achieve any measure of value, she had relied on her beauty, excellent shooting skills and perfect record of secretly sneaking into different targets' beds, killing them, and leaving without a trace.

Lana turned to face Cal and ran her fingers through his hair, trailing them down his face, and nestling them into his thick chest hair. "Are all American men like you?"

All her life, she had been taught American men were evil infidels, and the women were disgraceful harlots. It was her Islamic duty to kill all those who didn't believe in true Islam, seeking martyrdom for the cause of Allah, which would guarantee her entry into the heavenly kingdom.

She had questioned those beliefs so many times during her brief stay in America. She witnessed Christians, Jews, Muslims, atheists, agnostics, and people of all faiths, working and living together in peace. She had experienced nothing but kindness from those she was told to hate. The peace and safety she experienced while staying with Cal was the only respite from violence she had ever known.

Cal gently kissed her lips. "Only men who are lucky enough to have someone like you in their lives. So, what do you think about meeting my parents?"

Lana closed her eyes and wondered what would happen to Cal at the end of this day. He had welcomed her into his home so easily, and believed everything she told him. They had grown so close. She knew he would be heartbroken when he learned the truth.

She would miss being loved by him, having her opinions respected, being asked what she wanted, living as if her life mattered. She shook away her American daydreams and rolled out of bed.

"When my English is better, I meet your parents. But today, I have to do this. I have people depending on me."

"*I* depend on you," Cal said with a pout.

She fought the urge to crawl back in bed. She was one of a small group of ISIL women trusted to come to America. She must do this for those left behind who were no more than vehicles to detonate bombs. If she could prove she had value, maybe she could somehow stay in this country.

Lana stepped into the shower and relished the hot water and creamy body wash. She massaged an ample amount of shampoo into her hair, savoring the private bathroom filled with American toiletries. The smooth razor glided over her leg, leaving her feeling decadent.

Cal slipped into the shower and slid his arms around her waist. "Why are you showering before you go run?"

She hesitated and smiled. "Because I can." She turned and kissed him, reigniting their passion one last time.

After their shower, Cal sat on the bed with a towel wrapped around his waist and watched Lana wiggle into a pair of black spandex running pants. "I'm done with finals at 10:00. Call me if you want to meet for lunch."

She gave Cal a final kiss and snagged her backpack on the way out the door to the Metro.

Cal kissed her good-bye. "You are the sweetest, most wonderful woman in the world."

Lana smiled innocently back at him. Looks had never been so deceiving.

A wave of giddiness surged through Lana over the American freedom to leave the house by herself, wear what she wanted, and go wherever she wanted.

All thoughts of freedom were set aside. She reached into her backpack for her colored contacts, pulled out a pocket mirror, and changed her persona.

Her happy American mask disintegrated a bit more with every step closer to the Metro. Lana focused on the address she had memorized and steeled herself to do what must be done. It was as if she had mentally flipped a switch from girlfriend to terrorist when she stepped off the Washington Metro and headed to her first job. She was all business when she slipped in the back door of the first home. She would go in, assassinate her targets, and move on to her next job.

Chapter 2
Syrian Op #702

Monday, May 9th, 5:30 am.

Bill glanced at the clock—5:30 a.m. He glared across the hall through the glass wall at the model-shaped blonde with long, silky hair. Her lips were in a permanent pout, and her eyes were big and round, like an innocent child's.

Jessica sat with her legs and arms crossed and tried to ignore Bill's intermittent glares from across the hall. She had been his Special Assistant for three years. Before that, she was an agent in the Washington field office.

She stifled a yawn and took another gulp of coffee. She had worked through the night, trying to decipher whether the ISIL threat was to DC or a specific Syrian operation. She read an email from her neighbor/dog walker while she waited for the representatives from DC Metro and the Capitol Police to leave her boss's office.

Hey Jessica,

I think Jeb is mad at you for not coming home. He destroyed your new blinds. I'll check on him a little later, and will probably take him with me to my mom's if you don't make it back. She loves seeing him.

Jessica reread the email. Jeb was a well-trained Lab who had never torn up anything in her townhouse. She sighed with frustration. It had taken her a year to finally get around to putting up new blinds. She dismissed the thought when she saw the men clear her boss's office.

She jumped up and rapped on the door under his nameplate—Bill Carr, Assistant Director. "Sir. I've met with the Washington field office and CONUS 2 personnel (Continental U.S.–Section 2). The validity of the threat is still undetermined. I have the briefs from your meetings with Homeland Security and the CIA. I've sent the names and selectors to CT Watch (Counterterrorism), and they are scrubbing databases for derogatory information."

"Come in, I want to talk to you before my next briefing."

Jessica tucked the file under her arm and approached Bill's desk. "Yes, sir."

Bill leaned forward and rubbed his hand over his morning stubble. "Sit down. We've got five minutes before my next meeting. We're going to go over this one more time. I've talked to every law enforcement branch in DC in the past eight hours. No one else has received information about this threat. The only thing we know for sure is that your name was logged in on the very day before we received it."

He spread his hand menacingly over the piece of paper that threatened retaliation for the Syrian Operation #702 by killing each name on the list, as well as their families. His voice rose with every syllable he spoke. "And right now my butt is on the line, not to mention our national security is at risk. We've got to get ahead of this, *now*. If someone can break the encryption on that file, they can break into *any* government file."

"Sir, we have been over this, and my answers haven't changed."

Bill, who was usually calm and analytical in his dealings, pounded his fist on the desk, and Jessica jumped. "DO YOU THINK THIS IS SOME KIND OF GAME? We aren't just dealing with the OPM (Office of Personnel Management) hack anymore."

Bill wadded up the sheet of paper listing nine names involved in an ongoing classified Syrian Op #702 and threw it across his desk. "This operation is highly classified. This is way more than a government hack. We are talking about a government leak—a mole. Someone has to have leaked sophisticated, encrypted passwords to breach that file. Innocent civilians may be killed, and that includes *our* families."

"I've told you everything I know!"

"DAMMIT! We are running out of time! Four people have access to that restricted file, and the only two who have *ever* logged in are sitting right here." He mentally kicked himself for not following up on the alert. He had become lax. He should have checked the activity when he was sent an alert that she had accessed the file. His carelessness allowed him to be exploited.

"Why do you think *I* leaked the file? Why can't you believe in the possibility that it was hacked?"

"Oh, I can believe it was hacked. I think you helped."

Jessica threw her shoulders back and straightened her posture. "No, sir. You're wrong. But, just for the sake of discussion, how do you propose I did it?"

"Your name was logged in. Are you saying it wasn't you?" He assessed her reaction and analyzed her inflections. She was lying, and he knew it. He curled his hand into a fist, stifling the urge to slap a confession out of her.

Bill was a former Hostage Rescue Team Operator, HRT, who had transferred out after his only daughter barely recognized him when he showed up as a surprise to her tenth birthday party. He had climbed the ladder fast in the FBI, and was an Assistant Director, but his time spent in the field had made him callous to pleas for mercy, and had forced him to get creative when he had to force confessions from the enemy.

A knock at the door slowed his anger's momentum. "What is it?" he shouted.

His secretary stood in the doorway with pursed lips. "Sir, your next appointment is here."

Jessica left the room and scurried to the elevator to gather more intelligence.

***

It was still dark when Lana stepped off the metro and jogged into the upscale Alexandria neighborhood. She paused in front of the address she had memorized and bent down next to a bush, pretending to tie her shoe. Her senses were on full alert as she scanned the perimeter for activity and stashed her backpack in the bushes. She took a deep breath to calm her nerves. This was the moment of truth. She slipped the list of names under a rock—the list would serve as her calling card—then slinked into the shadows and approached the back door.

The back door had a resin urn with a potted plant conveniently sitting next to the door. She tipped the planter, spotting the key exactly where Ahmed told her she would find it.

American targets weren't all that different from those in Syria—so predictable.

She slid the key out with her foot and let herself into the back door of the garage. Once inside, she heard scratching at the door. She slowly turned the doorknob, and a black and white pug terrier ran from the kitchen, demanding to be let outside. Lana opened the back door, and the dog bolted.

A bowl of fruit sat on the counter next to a basket of mail. A high chair was pulled close to the small, round table. She took the safety off her gun and checked the silencer. Stuffed animals lay on the floor in front of the television in the living room. Little shoes were on the sides of the stairs as she ascended. A floorboard creaked when she reached the top of the stairs. She stopped and listened. Nothing.

A door at the far right end of the hall had little pony stickers covering it. She pushed open the door and saw a little girl sleeping under a princess bedspread.

Her ISIL training kicked in, and she pushed the cold steel tip into the mass of dark curls cascading over her pillow. Her finger was on the trigger, but she hesitated to pull back. *What has this little girl ever done to deserve this?* ISIL leaders had drilled into them that they were to kill all non-believers. Americans are in Syria now killing their children, they said. They are infidels, they said. Her finger trembled on the trigger, and she swallowed the bile rising in her throat. She lowered the gun and walked to the next room. *I'll finish her on my way out.*

Sound bites of ISIL ideology drilled into her for the last eight years kept screaming at her to do her job. But *none* of that ideology described what she experienced in America. Where were these evil infidels? These were *children*. Where were the hateful people she was sent here to kill?

She pushed opened the door across the hall and approached a white crib with a mobile, dangling colorful little animals. A pink bundle of fleece with a pacifier was curled up in the corner next to a stuffed bunny. The bunny triggered memories of the one she was forced to leave behind with her mother. She ran her hand over the silky head and picked up the tiny infant, sniffing her baby-scented head. The giraffe night light backlit her reflection against a dozen small windowpanes as she rocked the baby in her arms. She stared at the many faces staring back at her and questioned which one she was. Tears stung the back of her eyes. She kissed the downy soft hair and pretended for an instant this was her life. Then she gently placed the soft bundle back in the crib.

She pulled her gun and pointed it at the baby. ISIL soldiers were trained to torture their victims. She rationalized that pulling the trigger would be merciful. *But this was a baby!*

She spotted the baby monitor and heard the mother stirring in the other room. She knew there would be serious consequences if she didn't take out her targets. That meant murdering this innocent family. She was the one who'd posted the kill list. This was her job; she had to prove herself.

She heard a toilet flush down the hall. Panic made her mouth go dry. *She couldn't do it.* Her heart was hammering as she put her gun away and raced down the stairs. The dog was scratching at the outside door. She opened the door, and he bolted past her to his bowl in the kitchen, nudging it in her direction, and barking to be fed. She slammed the kitchen door and was locking the outside door when the mother flipped on the outside light and yelled that she had called the police.

Lana dashed around the side of the house, grabbed her backpack, and jogged breathlessly back to the metro. She was overcome with shame while she waited on the platform for her train with the other early commuters. How could she even think of killing those children? Had America changed her so much? Would she have done that in Syria? No. Syria was different. It felt good to sink her knife into those evil men. It was survival. Do or die. But here, Americans had hopes and dreams, women were respected— something that was never possible in Syria.

She took a seat next to the window and stared out into the dark. What would happen now? Had she just signed her death certificate? Would they kill Cal to punish her? Would someone else be sent to do the job she didn't finish?

She was grateful they had agreed to go dark. There was to be no communication until they met later to assess the damage. She heaved a deep sigh and hoped this would give her time to think of a plausible explanation to give the other cell members for why her targets were still alive.

On the other side of DC, in Bethesda, another family wasn't so lucky.

***

Bill stood and walked the chief of Metro Security to the door. He could put a check mark on his list next to Metro Security. They were deploying bomb-sniffing dogs throughout the metro stations and adding more eyes on any packages. He reluctantly called his secretary. "Do you know where Jessica is?"

"Yes, sir. She is meeting with personnel to gather addresses. She said to let you know she will be back by 6:00 a.m."

Bill glanced at his watch, 5:55 a.m. "Okay, send her in as soon as she gets back, please."

"She's getting out of the elevator now."

Jessica's heels clicked across the floor to Bill's office. She tucked her hand into her pants pocket and leaned against the doorjamb. "You wanted to see me?"

"Yes. We need to get a plan in place for the families involved in this file."

"I just pulled their addresses. Two are here in the suburbs of DC—one in Bethesda, and the other in Alexandria. Three more are on a military base."

"Okay, let's get some security on those addresses today. Do we know any more about the threat?"

"Nothing conclusive. We have everyone on alert, and people will be in place today at specific locations to monitor suspicious activity."

Bill ran his hand down his face. "That's not much to present to the Deputy Director."

Jessica chewed the side of her lip. "It's the best we can do when we're looking for a needle in a haystack."

She yo-yoed in and out of the hot seat with Bill in between his appointments for almost thirty minutes. His terse replies kept their discussion short of an argument. They repeatedly combed through the same information with no real progress.

Jessica's eyes were glazing over from the repetitive conversation when a tall young man with an earpiece and dark suit appeared at Bill's door. "Sir. I'm sorry, but the Director has to brief the president at 0 900, and the Deputy Director would like to see you in his office at 0 800."

Bill glanced at the clock on the wall and swore under his breath. He gave Jessica a killer glare. His computer flashed an urgent message on his classified email. *In light of the recent intelligence threats to FBI and military families related to Operation #702, please ensure action this day to notify all persons referenced in the threat traffic.*

"We've got seven minutes before we have to give the Deputy Director a plausible explanation of why classified names and addresses are being targeted. Neither one of us is going to get out of this unscathed. We are the only two people who accessed that file. We were in charge of this, and we are the ones responsible. We need to work together."

Jessica threw up her arms. "And by working together, you mean throwing me under the bus?"

"DAMMIT! WHY CAN'T YOU SEE THIS FOR WHAT IT IS? THERE IS A BREACH, AND *WE* ARE RESPONSIBLE FOR THE CASE FILE!"

Jessica kicked her crossed leg back and forth while she maintained a calm expression. "I do see this for what it is. You seem to want to keep the focus on me. We need to come at this from different angles."

Six minutes later, Bill and Jessica were on their way upstairs to the Deputy Director's office. Jessica broke the deafening silence between them. "When was the last time you talked to the Deputy Director?"

Bill shrugged. "Last night."

"What did he say?"

"He told me he wanted an immediate resolution."

Jessica shivered at the idea of walking into the impending meeting without the slightest hint of a resolution. They stopped at the secretary's desk but were waved in by the Deputy Director. He put the phone down and stared at them.

"Bill. Jessica."

Bill cleared his throat. "Gene."

Jessica tipped her head in a slight nod. "Sir."

The Deputy Director held out his hand to accept the brown file folder from Bill. "What do you know?"

"We have a known threat claiming to be from ISIL. They have targeted specific names of FBI/CIA agents. We have confirmation those names match the cover sheet on the classified undercover Syrian Operation #702. We believe the covers of all five agents are blown. This op has sensitive information that may put the country at risk. We have no intelligence to suggest it has been disseminated yet."

He cleared his throat and continued. "IT has changed all passwords and is individually wiping all computers and checking for security leaks. We are chasing leads to local ISIL cells, and watching all lone wolves on file."

"Have you notified your families?"

Bill ran his hand down his tie. "No, sir. I just read the email."

"What about you, Jessica?"

"My parents are in Long Island, and my dad is retired from the NYPD and a staunch advocate of the NRA. He wouldn't listen if I tried to caution him." She half smiled and held up her palms. "So why worry them?"

A muscular man in an ill-fitting suit appeared in the doorway. "Excuse me, sir." He walked over and handed the Deputy Director a sheet of paper.

The DD's face fell, and he slowly placed the piece of paper on his desk along with his glasses. "It's started. Lt. Campbell—CIA undercover in Syria. His wife called the police on an attempted break-in. They found a list with her husband's name crossed off in pencil under a rock in the bushes at their Alexandria home."

Bill went white and looked like someone had punched him in the gut. "Anyone hurt?"

The DD shook his head. "Campbell's wife is shook up. She knows they were targeted. CIA is working now to get him out of Syria since his cover is blown. The other names on the list were marked off in black marker. Our guys say the list will match the names listed on the cover sheet in this file. Any guesses who got into your files, Bill?"

Jessica felt sick. The threat just got very real. She held her breath and waited for Bill to throw her under the bus.

Bill shook his head. "We've gone over every piece of this, and don't see where the breach could have occurred. Jessica and I are the only two who have logged into the file."

The Deputy Director leaned back in his chair. "We don't know where this is going, or how deep this breach is. All current intelligence suggests attacks will be targeted at those on the list. For now, let's put FEMA (Federal Emergency Management Agency) and the National Guard on alert. Metro is to step up surveillance and patrols. Put Metro police on every corner." He splayed his hands on his desk and sighed. "I'm going to brief the Director on the classified information and personnel involved. We will provide protection for the families and meet back here at 0 930. Go call your families."

Bill closed the door to his office and dialed home. *No answer*. He called Karen's cell phone. *Voicemail*. He checked the time, 9:00 a.m., and let out the breath he was holding. It occurred to him that, thanks to the frantic pace of the past twelve hours, he hadn't called Karen in at least that long.

He ran his fingers through his hair and closed his eyes when he remembered the special dinner she had planned last night. "She's pissed and not going to take my calls," he muttered.

Jessica burst through his door as he hung up. "Jennings' family was just found in Bethesda. All of them—the whole family—were executed, and the house was torched."

Bill ran his hand down his face. "*Shit!* Is there any hard evidence indicating this is a coordinated attack?"

Jessica nodded slowly. "ISIL claimed responsibility online and threatened there would be more to come. The same list—only with this target's name crossed off in pencil—was found again. And again, the other names were blacked out."

Bill handed Jessica a folder. "Get these updated."

He checked the time, 9:15 a.m. and texted 911 to Karen, then called again, and she answered.

After their brief conversation, he hung up, hoping she would realize the seriousness of the situation and follow his instructions. He walked to the hall and barked at his secretary. "Get Agent Marcs on the phone, *now*."

Five minutes later, Marcs was briefing Bill on the agent he was sending to meet his wife at the boat, and the other he'd assigned to find Bill's daughter, Emma. "Agent Garrison will be there within the half hour, sir."

"Liam Garrison?" Images of Garrison down at Quantico training ran through his mind. He was top in his class, expert marksman, and built for combat. Distrust gnawed at the edge of Bill's subconscious. *Was it because of the man's good looks and cocky attitude?*

"Yes, sir. He has his captain's license, and knows the local rivers and the Bay."

Bill ran his hand over his face and nodded. He didn't have time to analyze his gut instincts.

Chapter 3
BOB

Monday, May 9th, 8:35 a.m.

Karen squinted against the morning sun at the undisturbed covers on her husband, Bill's, side of the bed and was instantly annoyed. She glanced at the alarm clock, 8:35 a.m. Their marriage had been stale for a while, but if he was cheating…

Last night's conversation with Peggy, her neighbor and best friend, echoed in her mind. She'd called Peggy to come over last night, after another picture-perfect dinner sat waiting, without even the slightest consideration of a phone call from her husband. Peggy had come over with a bottle of wine, and they drank it with the roasted duck and grilled vegetables she had painstakingly prepared for Bill.

They sat around the pool on the patio discussing everything from their children and husbands to their new manicures. They had been friends for a long time, and they both had children attending Georgetown University—Peggy's eldest son, Cal, and Karen's only daughter, Emma. Peggy complained because Cal's new girlfriend was occupying all his time and attention. She hadn't heard from him in weeks.

Karen grabbed her robe and nonchalantly walked through the upstairs, glancing around for signs of where he slept. She checked the extra bedrooms. Nothing. Emma's room felt stuffy, so she opened the window and proceeded downstairs. No blankets on the couch or shoes on the floor. She peeked into the garage to find his car missing.

Her irritation morphed into anger. Peggy's words from last night kept whispering to her. "Bill is a handsome man. Good-looking men in his position have twenty-year-olds throwing themselves at them." Karen dismissed Peggy's insinuations at the time, chalking them up to Peggy's insecurities about her own unfaithful husband.

She slammed the garage door shut. *If he is cheating…*

The phone rang, and she saw Bill's name on the caller ID. *Screw him! Let him learn how it feels to wait for me for a change.* She ignored the call and poured the coffee grounds into the filter and filled the reservoir with water.

She glanced out at the pool and called Peggy to come over for coffee and lie out in the sun with her. The pool needed to be skimmed, so she changed into her skimpy swimsuit to catch some sun, grabbed a cup of coffee, and went outside. Raccoons had knocked over the empty wine bottle and glasses sitting on the small table between the chaise lounges—all that was left from her and Peggy's "bash Bill" session last night.

She slammed the debris from the skimmer against the concrete with a vengeance when her ringtone startled her, singing Pharrell William's, "I'm so happy…" She tossed the pole aside and stomped over to her phone, suspecting it was Bill. She stared at the caller ID—Bill. *Jerk.*

She rolled her eyes and planned to ignore his call again, but before she could return to pulverizing the debris from the pool, a text chimed. She glanced at the screen, and it read 911!! It was from Bill. She noted the time—9:15 a.m.

The phone rang while she was reading the text. "Hello?"

Bill's voice was controlled, with a strong overtone of urgency. "Karen, if you have *a few seconds*, could you pick up Bob and Grace and meet at Mike's in an hour?"

Karen was caught off guard. She was wondering who Bob and Grace were until it struck her. BOB was code for Bug Out Bag, and he was referring to Grace, their forty-foot trawler. Mike was their friend on the South River who owned The Crab House.

"And can you clean out the kitty's bowl before you leave?"

Her stomach dropped; they didn't have a cat. He meant for her to get some money. That meant they would be gone for a while.

"Uh…okay…uh…"

"Oh, and I'm sorry, I broke your phone, so we'll need to get you a new one. Just *leave yours on the counter.*"

Obviously, she was using her phone, so it wasn't broken. The implication was that someone was listening to the call.

Her frantic thoughts immediately focused on her daughter. *Does she know?* "I was wondering if you've talked to Emma today?"

He seemed to hesitate as a silent pause settled on the line. "No."

"Should I call her?"

"You don't have time now, BOB's waiting on you." His voice was dead serious. "Karen…don't trust anyone." *Click.* The line went dead.

She pushed aside the shock to concentrate on his message. Get the bug-out-bag (BOB), clean out our bank account, and motor Grace, the trawler, over to the pier at The Crab House—a restaurant owned by their friend Mike. But he hadn't reached Emma.

She threw the phone down like it was a snake that had just bitten her. Her thoughts scrambled in every direction while she chased after them and raced upstairs to grab the BOB bag from her closet.

The national news had been reporting the hacked personnel files of all government employees for the past week. Bill and she had discussed how the breach could affect them. If the wrong people obtained the right information, they could steal his identity and wreak havoc with their finances. But what could be so serious that she had to run?

Bill's job had always kept him looking over his shoulder. The sensitive nature of his cases caused him to be overly protective of his family, and consequently, they devised a plan for what to do in the worst-case scenario. They had discussed it many times over the years, and they all knew the drill, but she never thought they would use it. Time to implement the plan.

She needed to warn Emma. The landline was next to the bed. Bill's words replayed in her head that she had seconds to get out of the house. *What's happened?* She bit her lip and decided to call.

When she got Emma's voicemail, she left a quick message. "Emma, meet me at the boat. If I'm not there, go to The Crab House."

She reached one hand into the back of her closet for the BOB bag and was surprised by its weight. She never thought she'd actually use the BOB. It was just something she put together for a worst-case scenario—a fire or an emergency. A great deal of time and meticulous planning had been invested in filling it with supplies over the past year in the event the worst happened. It contained a myriad of small, travel-size necessities, survival gear, and other items she'd randomly added to a backpack when she saw something that might be useful. She used both hands to lift the bag, balancing it on her back using the shoulder straps.

She struggled with the lock on the fire safe, grabbed their passports then glanced at the alarm clock, 9:20 a.m. Fifty-five minutes left. "I need more than this!" Her internal emergency alert system started screaming, "*Buy it later, get out NOW!*

She fumbled with the BOB bag, unable to stop herself from grabbing more things on the way out the door. She spotted a cloth grocery bag and picked up her phone—*he told me to leave it*. It was counterintuitive to leave the phone on the counter, but she knew he meant for her to leave it behind. She stuffed a T-shirt, shorts, laptop, charger and sunglasses into the reusable bag.

The garage door screeched open, and she spotted a cable van parked in front of her house. She ignored the two young men climbing out of the van and started piling her bags in the back of the SUV.

The two men turned around when they spotted Peggy moseying over in her swimsuit cover-up and towel.

Peggy had her hair pulled back in a ponytail and carried a small cooler. "Hey, Karen. Where's the fire? I thought we were going to lie out at the pool this morning?"

Karen glanced at her watch, 9:23 a.m. "Oh. Hey, Peggy, I totally forgot. I'm sorry, but I'm late for an appointment."

Peggy raised her eyebrows and looked like she swallowed a bug. "You going like that?"

She forgot she was in the middle of skimming the pool five minutes ago in a tiny swimsuit and flip-flops. She glanced down, pulling her bottoms up to cover her flabby stomach, which was now hanging over the skimpy bottoms, and tucking her boobs back into the flimsy top. "I…I…gotta go."

Peggy gaped at her from the driveway while Karen waved at her in the rearview mirror and sped away. She approached the cable van and stopped them as they began to pull away. "Hey, are you looking for a certain address?"

The two young men appeared anxious and confused. "No. We…we forgot something."

Peggy narrowed her brows in confusion. "Were you coming to this address? We are the only two houses on this cul-de-sac."

The driver of the van was glancing impatiently at his rearview mirror.

Peggy rested her hand on the open window. "Were you going to my neighbor's house?"

Sweat was dripping from the young man's forehead in the passenger seat. "No. We have to go now."

The driver screeched away from the curb and yelled at the other. "You idiot! We've lost our target thanks to your fucking chit-chat!"

"I was trying to avoid arousing suspicion."

Karen's heart was pounding, and her mind was darting through every dark scenario hidden in the corners of her imagination. She flipped on the radio.

The newscaster's voice was grave and laced with fear. "Breaking news. A woman and her children were discovered in their burning home in Bethesda. Firefighters have contained the flames and say it has suspicious origins.

"Neighbors say the house belongs to a military family consisting of a wife and two small children. The husband is deployed overseas.

"There are FBI agents with the ERT (Evidence Response Team) here working with the fire marshal. There are strong rumors that this fire was set deliberately."

Karen gasped and shut off the radio, trying to rein in her imagination. Her insides were turning to liquid. *How am I going to contact Emma? Surely Bill is working on it.* Her daughter was packing up her college apartment for the summer, and would be heading home any day.

9:30 a.m. Her stomach dropped, and she smacked her trembling hand against the steering wheel when she screeched into the bank's parking lot and saw the long lines at the bank's drive-thru windows. She shimmied into a T-shirt and shorts then slammed the car door behind her before walking into the bank.

She handed the teller two checks, one for the money market, and one for the checking. "I'd like to close these accounts in cash, please."

Everything seemed to move in slow motion, especially the clock, when the young girl came back to the counter. "I'm sorry. I'll need to get my supervisor to approve this transaction, and she's with another customer."

The clock on the wall over the girl's shoulder registered 9:35 a.m. She had forty more minutes. *I'll never make it.* "Okay, I understand. I'm in a bit of a hurry."

"I have to have her signature for any cash withdrawals over five thousand."

"Well, what about if I take five thousand in cash, and you can write a check for the rest?"

She smiled sweetly and seemed relieved not to have to interrupt her supervisor. "Okay. I can do that."

9:45 a.m. Fifteen minutes after she arrived at the bank, Karen pulled into traffic and headed to the marina. Her stomach dropped as she forced herself to listen to the woman's voice on the radio. "It's no coincidence. We are standing outside a home today in a quiet suburb of Alexandria. We earlier reported the fire in Bethesda. This is the second family today, both of them government employees, who have been targeted in their homes.

"This family, a wife, a little girl, and a baby—was lucky. Their dog scared away a person trying to break into their home. Neighbors say a list of names was found in front of the house with her husband's name crossed out. Whoever planned to break into this home was targeting the family because of her husband, who is stationed overseas."

"These are exactly the kinds of cowardly acts that have been threatened by ISIL against our military and police. They target the defenseless families for easy victims and use their deaths to spread fear. An investigation is underway to find a link to the house fire in Bethesda earlier today. Authorities say they have no leads at this time."

Karen punched the dial off. She'd heard enough—any more dreadful news, and she was going to lose it. Paranoia set in. She glanced at the dashboard clock, 9:55. *They'll know my car.* Glancing in the rearview mirror, she didn't see anyone following her, but to be sure, she drove past the marina entrance and pulled a U-turn in a parking lot. The slip owners' lot was half full when she backed into a space and sat waiting until she was reasonably sure no one had followed her, then shut off the car and grabbed a cart.

After several furtive glances over her shoulder, she felt semi-sure she was alone. She threw the other BOB bag that they kept in the car into the cart, along with the contents of the glove compartment and console, and walked briskly toward the pier.

Thank God there was not much wind. It would be her saving grace. She lifted the contents of the cart onto the deck of the forty-foot trawler and tried to remember the routine. This was the first time she'd ever backed a boat of that size away from the dock by herself. *Okay. I can do this.* She quickly tossed the bags into the main cabin and started the engines, then ticked off the steps like a pilot at takeoff. Remove windshield cover, disconnect power cable, check wind and direction, take the bow lines, leave the stern lines.

10:00 a.m. Fifteen more minutes to meet Bill at The Crab House's dock, and no phone. She took a deep breath and jumped back on the dock, untying lines and throwing them back on the boat.

The woman who kept her boat in the slip next to theirs, Rondie, was retired FBI, and a veteran sailor. She popped up from her cabin and walked across the bow of her boat. "Some guy was just here asking about Bill."

Karen froze and braced herself for the next blow. "What guy? What did he look like?"

"Big. Beefy. Military, maybe. He wore a sleeveless black T-shirt with cargo shorts, hiking sandals and a broad-brimmed boater's hat. He was carrying a large black rucksack, stuffed full. Expensive gear."

Karen took a deep, calming breath and scanned the dock. "What did he say?"

"Asked if this was Bill Carr's boat. I asked him if he was a friend of Bill's and he just kinda glared at me and left. Where *is* Bill?"

Karen smiled and tried to sound casual. "I'm meeting him. It's just me today."

Rondie's eyes narrowed. "You need some help?"

Karen's gut told her Rondie suspected. "Yes. I've never taken this boat out on my own."

"Are you putting the lines *on* the boat?" Rondie's question was weighted with implication. The only reason she'd be untying the pilings and cleats is if she would need them to tie up elsewhere.

Their eyes locked in silent understanding. Karen swallowed hard. "Yes."

Rondie scrambled off her boat and helped her untie the rest of the lines. "I'll take this cart back for you." She paused and stared at Karen. "Do you need anything else?"

Karen saw the comprehension in Rondie's eyes. "Can I borrow your phone?"

Rondie pulled her phone from her back pocket. "Absolutely. Let me get the charger." She was back in seconds handing the charger over her boat's railing.

Karen swallowed the lump in her throat and blinked tears of gratitude. "Thank you. I will get this back to you as soon as I can."

"Don't worry about it." She shooed her hands. "Go. Good luck."

Karen climbed up to the flying bridge and shifted the engines into reverse. Her shoulders were hunched and her face pinched as she listened to the screeching from the forty-foot trawler scraping and banging against the pilings while she backed out. Rondie stood on the back of her boat with her arms crossed and jaw clenched while she watched the clumsy exit. Her worried grimace didn't inspire much confidence in Karen. Once she cleared the slip, she gave Rondie a hurried wave and focused on maneuvering around moored sailboats out to the channel.

Karen breathed a sigh of relief once she was in the river. 10:10 a.m. Five minutes. There was no way. Bill would just have to wait. She fished Rondie's phone from her pocket and dialed Emma again. She hung up when it went straight to voicemail. *Where is she?*

She punched at the buttons on the GPS and depth finder until the map popped up. She stared at the red and green buoy markers and regretted making fun of Bill's repeated attempts to teach her to drive the boat. "What was that stupid rhyme about which side of the buoy I'm supposed to be on? Red right return, black port on entering?" *Is that right? It can't be right; it doesn't rhyme.*

The depth finder was quickly dropping from twenty feet to twelve. She needed to be on the left of the green buoy heading out. She corrected her course, and the depth increased.

"Oh shit!" Two sailboats were tacking all over the place in front of her. *Who has the right of way?* She wanted to blow the horn and yell at them to get the hell out of the way. "How is anybody supposed to know what you're doing? Why don't boats have turn signals? It would make this so much easier." *Think, think, think!*

Before she could figure out the proper protocol, the people on the sailboat were waving their middle fingers and shouting obscenities as they narrowly missed the bow. She turned her palms up and mouthed a sincere apology, but what could she do? She had maybe five more minutes to motor up the Bay and cross over into the South River to meet Bill. It wasn't happening. When she reached the mouth of the river, there were hundreds of crab pots to maneuver around. She didn't have the time to finesse her way around them, so she just did her best to zigzag through the field of colorful little buoys marking the pots and prayed she didn't hook one.

She let go of the breath she didn't realize she was holding and eased into the Bay. She was zooming the map on the GPS to try to get her bearings when four deafening air horn blasts sounded from behind. She about jumped out of her skin at the warning blasts. When she turned toward the horn, she was looking straight up the front of a massive barge being pushed by a tug.

Where did that come from? She jerked the wheel away from the barge and gunned the engines, only to be confronted by a sailboat filled with kids hanging off the sides with beers in hand. She was only yards away from running right into them, and they were under sail, with no power or wind. The barge was coming along on the other side and was still blasting its horn.

Karen cut back the engines to hopefully lessen the impact. She closed her eyes and braced for the worst, but when she opened them, miraculously, the sailboat just missed sideswiping the stern, and the barge was a few yards ahead of her.

She glanced at the clock, 10:25 a.m. Her hour was over, and she was at least fifteen minutes away from The Crab House. Huge freighters were anchored randomly across the Bay, and a large cruise ship was coming south on her right. She set a straight course and headed toward the next river when the Coast Guard inflatable came out of nowhere with machine guns drawn screaming on a loud megaphone to stay five hundred feet away from the cruise ship. *Are you kidding?!* They were herding her to veer left.

Karen's hands were cramping from holding the wheel so tight, and every muscle in her body was beginning to scream from tension. The South River was coming up, and she would finally be able to get out of the Chesapeake Bay of Crazies.

"Another field of crab pots!" She was beyond caring. She bulldozed through the pots, daring them to snag the boat. "Red right return. Okay." She maneuvered the boat around, so the red buoys were on her right, and monitored the depth finder and chart upstream through the Route 2 Bridge until the Crab House came into view.

It hadn't occurred to her until that moment to think about how she was going to dock the boat in one of the tiny restaurant slips. She cut the engines to a crawl and searched the docks for Bill. Nothing. Where *the hell* was he?

She scanned the piers, restaurant, and people. No Bill. Her stomach dropped when she spotted the Tiki Bar and saw a man fitting the description of the beefy guy Rondie saw back at the slip. He locked eyes with her, hitched his rucksack over his shoulder, and started down the long pier.

Crap! Do I turn around? Head back out to the bay? Let him approach the boat? Did Bill send him? The gun! It's taped under the chair in the cabin. Her palms were sweating while she eased the engines into neutral and positioned the boat in an open area of water long enough to run down and grab the gun.

Mr. Military was increasing his pace and intensifying his stare. He seemed to be gauging Karen's moves.

She jumped down the bridge stairs onto the outside deck and scrambled into the main cabin, kicking the small leather club chair over on its side. She grabbed the lower controls from inside the cabin and straightened out the boat before ripping the gun from the bottom of the chair. She tucked the gun into the elastic waistband of her shorts and eased the boat along the pilings at the end of the dock, shifting it into neutral a good five feet away from the dock—far enough away so Mr. Military couldn't board.

Mr. Military was standing on the end of the pier glaring at Karen.

Her legs were shaking under false bravado while she raced back up to take the helm on the bridge so she could stare down at him. "Can I help you with something?"

His feet were set in a firm stance, and his eyes were hidden behind black wrap-around reflective sunglasses. He adjusted his rucksack and pulled his badge from his pocket. "We can't do this here." His voice was low and commanding.

Karen glanced over Mr. Military's head and down the forty-yard pier at the crowd eating at tables under brightly colored umbrellas. She caught the eye of Emma's friend, who was waitressing, standing at the table of two scruffy-looking twentysomethings dressed in long swim trunks and T-shirts, with greasy dark hair. She went to Georgetown with her daughter, and they would be waitressing together for the summer when Emma finished with classes. She was staring at Karen, shaking her head slowly. *What was she trying to communicate?* Bill's last words echoed in her mind. *Don't trust anyone.*

Karen's voice rose along with her eyebrows. "*We're* not doing *anything, anywhere* until I know what is going on."

Mr. Military had reflexes like a cobra. She'd completely underestimated him. In one swift move, he leaped onto the stern and was standing on the outside deck at the bottom rung of the bridge's short ladder. He reached forward and grabbed her ankle, making her stumble, and causing the baby Glock to drop through her shorts and land at her feet. He reached forward, picked up the gun, and tucked it in the back of his shorts, while keeping a firm hold on Karen's ankle.

In the next moment, he was beside her at the bridge's helm with his arms around hers in a vise grip. She couldn't move. He had pinned her arms to her sides.

"Be cool. I'm on your side. We have a large audience. Just act like you are greeting your lover."

Karen struggled to pull back from him, but his arms tightened.

"I'm going to let you go, and you are going to smile and lead me down into the cabin."

Fear turned her legs to jelly, and her ribs were screaming for relief. Her breaths were coming so hard and fast she thought she might hyperventilate or pass out. His steel grip was digging into her shoulder while she descended the ladder. The sheer strength in his arm over her shoulder warned her she'd better stick strictly to his orders.

Once in the main cabin, she narrowed her eyes and sneered. She shrugged off his arm and started to run out of the cabin to the outside deck.

His arms of steel wrapped around Karen's waist and lifted her a foot off the ground, leaving her running in thin air. "Whoa. Just chill. I'm FBI. I was sent to collect you."

Her ribs were howling under his crushing embrace. "I can't breathe! Let go of me! Where's my husband?"

The boat was knocking against the pilings and drifting toward the restaurant marina.

"Grab the wheel or let go of me!"

He took the wheel with one hand, steering it toward the river before shifting the engines into gear. His other arm was crushing her ribs as she struggled against him. "I want to let you go, but I'll handcuff you if I can't trust you."

Only dogs could hear Karen's high-pitched hysteria. "Can't trust *ME?*"

Mr. Military winced as her screams pierced his ears. He handled her like a sack of potatoes and plunked her down the four stairs to the galley, dumping her onto the bench in the little booth.

She inhaled deeply and rubbed her arms while he leapt back up to take the helm in the salon. "What is going on?"

"Karen. The Bureau sent me because your husband is stuck in traffic." He reached for Karen's gun in the back of his shorts and checked the safety. He smirked. "You know, these only work if they have bullets in them." He tossed her gun onto the cushion next to her.

She crossed her arms and returned his alpha tone. "Who are you? What's happened? Where are we going?"

Chapter 4
Emma

Monday, May 9th, 12:00 p.m.

Relief rolled off Emma in waves after she turned in her last final and hit the concrete outside of the Hariri Building. She knew she'd done well on all her exams and was giddy at the thought of being out of school for the summer.

"Emma! Emma Carr!"

Emma shaded her eyes at the hulking figure walking toward her. She gave him a big hug. "Blake! Are you finished with finals?"

"Yeah. A bunch of us are headed over to Tombs. You wanna go?"

Emma adjusted her backpack on her shoulder. "Absolutely." Her phone rang just as she headed down West Street in Blake's car. She checked the caller ID, unknown caller. She knew her dad's number usually came across with that tag, but she wasn't ready to let her parents know she was finished with finals. She wanted to have some fun, and didn't want a lecture from him about the drive home. It was only noon; she'd call him later. She still had a few days left on her lease, and didn't want to move back home to Annapolis until the last minute. Her friends were all planning parties, and would be expecting her. Besides, she had booked two twelve-hour shifts waitressing during the upcoming Commissioning weekend. Her tips from waitressing that weekend alone would more than triple what she'd make if she went home today and waitressed all week.

She tucked her phone into her back pocket and ignored the call. The bar was loud and filled with fellow students. They followed their friends wave to a table, zigzagging through the crowded bar and ordered another pitcher of beer.

She and Blake had dated for almost a year. He was 6' 3" and played on the lacrosse team, but his athletic commitments often conflicted with the amount of attention Emma was used to receiving as an only child of two doting parents.

Her friend Maggie leaned over to Emma and whispered loudly in her ear. "Check out the tall, dark, and handsome hottie at the bar. He's been staring over this way since you came in."

Emma nonchalantly rubbed her chin on her shoulder sneaking a peek at the bar. "That's my neighbor, Cal." She offered him a casual wave, and he gave her a half nod, continuing to play with his phone while he sat at the bar.

"I've met all your neighbors, and *he* is not your neighbor."

"His family lives next to my parents in Annapolis. He's not there much. He's older. I think he has an apartment around here. He's really smart. I think he's working on a masters or doctorate in chemistry or something. I know his little brother better."

Maggie stared at his curly black hair and thick shadow of a beard. She stroked at the imaginary beard on her chin and said, "He looks like he could be a terrorist."

"That's racist. They're a very nice family. The kids are brilliant. His younger brother is an honor student at South River High School. He mows our lawn and shovels drives in the winter—they're a very hard-working family."

Maggie threw up her hands in surrender as a shapely blonde settled onto the barstool next to Cal. "Well, damn, it looks like he has a girlfriend."

Emma remembered when Cal moved in around ten years ago. She had the biggest crush on him, but he never gave her the time of day, although she didn't take it personally. He had always been a loner.

Maggie elbowed Emma out of her thoughts. "So, how do you think you did on that Poly Sci final?"

The conversation drifted toward grades, summer jobs, and drinking games.

A few hours later, Blake held up his phone to Emma. "Why is your dad calling *me*?"

Emma picked up his phone and listened to the voicemail. "Blake, I'm trying to get a hold of Emma. If you see her, could you have her call me?"

"That's weird—probably because I ignored his call. I don't want them to know finals are over yet, or they'll make me go home."

Blake shrugged and stuffed his phone into his back pocket.

Emma pulled hers from her backpack and noticed there were nine missed calls. She sobered quickly when she pulled up the text to read 911!! She clicked on the voicemail from her mother earlier and heard the fear in her voice while she told her to go to the boat immediately.

Her dad's lectures and family emergency plans raced through her thoughts. She dialed his number, but got his voicemail. "Dad. What's going on? Call me back." She dialed her mom's cell and got her voicemail. "Mom. I can't get ahold of Dad. What's going on?" Her dad's lectures repeated over and over in her head. *Don't stop for anyone or anything, just get to the boat.*

The TV on the back wall showed an anchorwoman delivering breaking news. She called out to the bartender, "Hey, can you turn that up?"

Emma inched closer while she listened to what had happened to two families in the DC area who allegedly had been targeted by ISIL according to online claims. She watched while a house engulfed in flames was hosed down, and hysterical neighbors were interviewed.

Blake watched Emma's face drain of color. "What's the matter?"

Emma's stomach rolled, and her skin burned. She checked the time, 1:50 p.m. "I need to get my car. Can you give me a ride back to my apartment?"

"Yeah. Sure. What's going on?"

"I don't know. But I need to go home. Right now."

Blake double-parked outside Emma's apartment. Emma stopped abruptly with her hand on the car door handle. "Look. The front door is open."

"Maybe it's your roommate."

"She left yesterday."

"Maybe it's the sublets." He put his hand on her forearm. "I'll go see. You stay in the car."

Blake left the car double-parked with the key in the ignition and gently pushed open the front door. "Hellooo. Carrie?"

Emma turned off the car and followed Blake. "I told you she left."

Blake frowned at Emma for not staying in the car and put his finger over his lips. "Shh." He stepped inside and caught a glimpse of a hooded male running out the back kitchen door. He bolted after him and yelled at Emma to call the police.

Emma glanced around the apartment at the half-packed boxes and suitcases, fumbling with her phone while dialing 911.

"911. What's your emergency?"

"My boyfriend just ran after a guy who was in my apartment." She was in the middle of giving the pertinent information to the dispatcher when the phone was jerked from her hand, and an arm clamped around her like a vise. A scratchy burlap bag reeking of rotten garbage was forced over her head, and someone started dragging her using a chokehold. She was thrown into her hall closet, and the door slammed behind her. Muffled voices were outside the door. She gagged at the putrid-smelling slime that touched her face and tore the bag off her head. She leaned forward and peeked through the small gap between the door and the doorjamb.

She saw a hooded guy walk into the kitchen from the alley with something in his hand.

The creep who grabbed her asked, "Where's the guy?"

The hooded guy lifted a long bloody knife and waved it across his neck, then wiped it on her last clean dishtowel. "One problem solved. I threw him behind a bunch of garbage bags in the alley. Where's the girl?"

He jerked his thumb back over his shoulder. "In the closet. I think she called the police; we've got to get out of here, *now*."

Emma's heart hammered in her ears. Her mind was racing in survival mode. She felt around the closet for a weapon, and her hand landed on the BOB bag her dad had insisted she keep. She wrapped her hand around the wasp spray tucked into an outside pocket and searched for more weapons.

"We leaving the girl?"

"Hell, no! We're not letting her out of our sight. Our orders are to get the girl. We're making a little video with this one. Leaving her now is *not* an option! Let's get her in the van. She's been drinking all afternoon, and she's small. Didn't take much to put her in the closet. You get the van, and I'll meet you in the alley."

"Yeah. Okay."

Emma's adrenaline spiked. She hitched the BOB bag over her shoulder and waited for the door to open. The second she caught sight of him, she squirted the wasp spray directly into his eyes.

He stumbled back screaming and clawing at his eyes.

Emma grabbed the fire extinguisher and aimed for the head. *Thud. Nailed it.* He bent over, and she swung the broom handle between his legs. *Right on target!*

He dropped to the floor, out of breath, and bellowing with pain.

She grabbed her phone off the floor and ran for the front door without her car keys. She was torn between Blake and her escape. Her survival instincts forced her out the front door, away from the guy writhing in pain on the floor, and into Blake's car. She turned over the ignition and heard the sirens coming in her direction. *Please God, let them get to Blake in time.*

Chapter 5
Mr. Military

Monday, May 9th, 11:45 a.m.

Mr. Military stood at the cabin wheel, constantly scanning the periphery, and Karen sat a few steps down in the galley while they motored down the river to the bay.

Karen grabbed a couple bottles of water from the galley refrigerator and held one up to Mr. Military. "Water?"

"Thanks." He accepted the water and gulped it down, crushing the empty plastic. A wide charming smile lit his face. "Do you recycle?"

Karen took the empty bottle and tossed it under the sink. "Well, are you going to explain who you are and what is going on?"

"I tried earlier, but you didn't seem to be in the mood to listen."

Karen took a sip and glared at him. "Start talking."

"Have you talked to your husband today?"

She took another sip and stared at him without answering.

Mr. Military looked over his shoulder at the sound of fast approaching engines. "Get down! Get under the table."

Two jet skis were approaching the boat from behind. Karen peeked out the porthole and recognized the two scruffy-looking twentysomethings from the restaurant.

Mr. Military turned the wheel hard to the left, knocking one of them off his jet ski. "Get down, and for God's sake stay away from the windows!"

Unsecured items were rolling to the floor, and the boat was pitching against the waves. A loud thud against the boat's hull sent her fleeing under the table. The surprisingly loud bang of Mr. Military's pistol sent a cold shiver down her spine. One of the guys had been thrown into the water and was swimming toward his jet ski. The other was trying to pull up next to the ladder.

Mr. Military pointed his gun at the jet ski approaching the ladder. "Don't try it. This next bullet has your name on it."

Karen grabbed the wheel and made another sharp turn, creating a wave, and moving the unoccupied jet ski farther from its rider. The other guy lost his grip on the ladder and was forced to balance both hands on his jet ski or risk falling into the water. Karen wrenched the wheel in the opposite direction to avoid an oncoming sailboat. She flinched and ducked at the same time when more gunshots cracked.

Mr. Military had shot a neat pattern into the empty jet ski, and it was smoking. He yelled at Karen, "Doesn't this thing go any faster?"

Karen shot back a look of irritation and flipped up her palms. "It's a trawler! It's not going to do much better than ten knots! Stop shooting! They don't have guns. You are going to get us killed or arrested." She pointed at a can of wasp spray rolling on the deck next to the chair. "Try that wasp spray, it'll go eighteen feet."

Mr. Military rolled his eyes and shook his head. "I've got this. Just steer the boat and keep it steady." He let the other jet ski approach the swim platform on the back of the boat and then gripped the top of the ladder and kicked both feet out, sending the second guy catapulting into the water with his friend. The key to the jet ski was attached to a bright-colored bobber, making it easily accessible. Mr. Military pulled the key from the ignition and waved good-bye to the dark-haired guy flailing around in the water.

He gently nudged Karen away from the wheel and steered the boat toward open water. "We need to go."

Karen's legs were shaking from adrenaline. "Go *where*? What. Is. Going. On?"

Mr. Military's eyes softened. He opened his mouth to say something, but his phone rang.

His entire demeanor changed to a formal voice and a militant stance. He held the phone to his ear and barked, "Osprey 1."

Karen strained her neck to listen to his conversation.

"Yes…No…Not had a chance yet…Negative…Will do." He placed his hand over his mouth and spoke harshly into the phone. "You shouldn't have called me on this phone." He tucked the phone back into his pocket and stared at Karen.

Mr. Military caught Karen's inquisitive stare and shrugged. "Just the supervisor checking on our progress."

Karen nodded and raised her brows, pretending to buy his story. She stood and softened her eyes, then asked pleadingly, "May I use your phone to call my daughter?"

"I'm sorry. We can't take a chance on this phone being traced by an unknown. We don't know who may be monitoring your daughter's cell phone."

Karen expected him to decline and lowered her brows in a scowl. "Well? Are you going to tell me what is going on?"

Mr. Military ran his fingers through his hair. "Do you trust me?"

Karen slowly contemplated her answer. *Did she have any choice?* "I want to. Do you have any identification?"

He cocked his head and studied her, then pulled out his credentials.

Karen read his name on the credentials he presented. "Okay, *Liam F. Garrison,* what's going on?"

Liam's nostrils flared, and he flexed his shoulders in a stretch. "What do you know about the cases your husband is working on?"

Karen gave a half shrug. "Not much. He hasn't been home much, and doesn't usually share his work with me, other than to comment when the media starts reporting whatever he's been working on."

He fidgeted with the wheel and checked the charts for a new course. He stared straight ahead and spoke in a nonchalant tone. "Have you noticed anything out of the ordinary going on with him?"

A blush crept up from Karen's neck to her cheeks. *Was he asking her if Bill was cheating?* "You obviously have something you want to know…just ask me."

"Has he made any new friends lately? Needed money? Any routine habits changed?"

Karen straightened the chair and picked up the loose items on the floor. She wanted to keep her cards close to her chest until she knew more. "Like I said, he hasn't been around much."

Liam sighed. "Has he discussed any of the cases he has been working on with you? Any at all, no matter how trivial?"

Karen sat forward on the couch and threw up her hands. "I don't know. Why?"

Liam braced his stance and slipped one hand into his pocket while keeping the other on the wheel. He glanced over his shoulder at Karen and sighed, then focused on something ahead in the distance. "There has been a security leak. Classified information is being disseminated that will put a lot of families of undercover agents at risk."

"Bill isn't an undercover agent."

"No, but he is one of very few who have clearance to information regarding a very sensitive operation. One of the families of an agent involved in that operation is dead, another one avoided certain death thanks to her dog, and we are collecting others whom we believe may be next."

"Is this about the family who died in a fire this morning outside DC?"

He nodded slowly. "Both agents, the one whose family died, and the one whose family had an intruder, were named in the classified file that was leaked."

"Why are they going after the families?"

"To send a clear message—that they aren't f…messing around."

"What's this about?"

"Karen, I couldn't tell you if I knew. I know it opened up Pandora's box when the government's personnel files were hacked. Somehow a classified op has been leaked, and the names of agents in that op have been compromised and their families targeted."

"So, you are telling me that you suspect Bill of leaking information?"

"I am saying I was sent to collect you, because someone is attacking families to force classified information out of a small group of agents."

"Do you know where my daughter is?"

"I know we had eyes on her earlier, but I haven't been updated on her whereabouts."

"What about Bill?"

Liam shrugged. "Don't know."

"Were you lying earlier when you said he was stuck in traffic?"

Liam pursed his lips and paused. "Yes."

Karen leaned against the couch and rested her arm along the back. "He didn't come home last night. I expected him for dinner, but he didn't call or come home. The last I heard from him was a couple of hours ago, when he called and told me to get out of the house and go to the boat. He said he'd meet me at the restaurant."

Liam glanced over his shoulder at the two specks in the distance, still flailing in the water next to the jet skis. "I wasn't the only one listening to that call, it appears."

"You don't know that. For all we know, those were two guys going after a woman they suspect was kidnapped by a guy that jumped on her boat!"

"Did you see their tats?"

Karen shook her head.

"Trust me, they are not the good guys."

"What's the plan then?"

Liam searched the different gauges. "Where's the gas gauge?"

Karen pointed down into the galley. "You have to pull away the stairs to the engine room. There is a dipstick that measures the tank level."

"Do you have any idea how much fuel is on board?"

Karen shrugged. "Not a clue, but it holds 300 gallons." She was relieved to have someone else to share the boat's responsibilities.

Chapter 6
Sierra Charlie

Monday, May 9th, 2:15 p.m.

Emma's white-knuckle grip on the wheel wasn't enough to stop her uncontrollable shaking. It took her four tries to punch in 911 while pulling into traffic.

"911. What's your emergency?"

"I called a minute ago. My boyfriend is stabbed in the alley and…" The phone died. She had left her purse behind, along with her charger and car keys. Her dad's words replayed in her head. *"Get to the boat, don't stop for anything."* Luckily, Blake's car charger was lying in the console. She plugged in her phone and weaved through traffic out of Georgetown.

A voice of reason told her Blake would be found shortly, and there was nothing she could do to help him. She pulled onto the beltway to put distance between her and the two men who were after her. Her gut instinct told her the two guys were related to the news.

Why did her parents text 911? Why aren't they returning her calls? The answers were terrifying her. A car sped up next to her and blared his horn at her for cutting him off when she changed lanes. *Focus. Concentrate on driving.*

She checked the rearview mirror, but didn't know what she should be looking for. Her mind kept whizzing back to Blake. She couldn't push away the image of the guy wiping Blake's blood from his knife—or the guilt from leaving him behind. She checked her phone, but still no charge. A voice inside her seemed to say *find your courage and be brave.*

She straightened her shoulders and channeled her inner badass. *I can do this.* She put her foot on the pedal and drove the beltway like it was the Indy 500, watching the rearview mirror and constantly glancing back over her shoulder, until she pulled into the marina forty-five minutes later.

Emma gathered her BOB bag and what few other belongings she had, and felt a measure of relief to be closer to home and her parents. *They would know what to do.* Her pace quickened as she hurried across the parking lot. Her resolve was crumbling, and she was on the verge of tears just knowing she was minutes away from the relief of seeing her parents.

Fear stunned her when she didn't see the flying bridge of their boat sticking out above the others. She ran down the dock and dropped her bags in front of the empty boat slip. She stared down the river searching for the boat until the last of her resolve crumbled and she collapsed next to her bags, dropping her head in her hands. "They're gone."

Rondie popped up through her boat hatch and walked toward her across the deck. "Hey, Emma, how ya doin'?"

Emma sniffed and looked up at Rondie through weepy eyes. "Hi, Rondie. I was hoping to catch Mom and Dad on the boat. Did you see them leave?"

Rondie bit her lip. She had tracked her phone on her computer all morning using her *Find My Phone App* while listening to the news, and pieced together a possible scenario. "I've got a number where you can reach your mom."

Emma stood and pulled her phone from her pocket. She wiped at the tears running down her cheeks. "What's the number?"

Rondie's eyes narrowed, and she climbed down from the boat. "Let's take a walk." She spoke in a low whisper while they walked down the pier. "You need to get rid of your phone. I think people are tracking your family, and your phone's GPS is giving them all the information they need. Ditch the phone and meet me back at my boat. I'll be ready to shove off when you get back. Hurry." Rondie checked her watch. 3:00 p.m.

As they approached the parking lot, police cars were pouring in from every direction. A cable van made a U-turn at the corner.

Emma bit her lip to fight back tears. Her voice was shaky. "What's going on?"

"I'm not sure, but I have some ideas." Rondie shaded her eyes and watched while the police surrounded Blake's car. "Do you know whose car that is?"

Emma's stomach dropped and she nodded. "My boyfriend, Blake's."

"Quick, find a busy place to leave your phone—a public restroom is good. Just lock it and leave it in a stall. Someone will turn it in, don't worry. Then meet me at the boat. I'll fill you in on what I know."

Five minutes later, Rondie was throwing the lines off the boat, Sierra Charlie, and pulling away from the pier. She hoisted the mainsail, leaving the jib down because of the approaching weather.

Rondie squared her shoulders and decided not to sugarcoat the news. "Did you drive that car here?"

Emma choked on a sob. "Yes. I was running from two guys. One stabbed Blake and I ran. Oh my God!" She bent over and sobbed into her hands. "What have I done? I left him there!"

Rondie gave her a sympathetic pat and maneuvered through the area between the marina and the channel, which was dotted with mooring buoys and their sailboats rocking in the wind. Dark clouds were approaching fast. She had to sail out of the West River to the bay, and then get over to the Severn River in order to reach the Annapolis harbor before the storm hit.

Disappearing in a busy harbor would be easy. Once they were in the channel, she asked, "Where's your boyfriend?"

"Back at my apartment. Two guys were waiting for me. Blake ran after one, and he was stabbed and left in the alley behind my apartment. I called 911, but my phone died. I didn't know what to do." Her shoulders shook as she caved to uncontrollable weeping. "I…need…to t-t-talk…to Mom and Dad," she said between sobs.

Rondie delivered the occasional comforting pat while she steered them out into the channel, figuring Emma needed to let her feelings out before they could get to the next steps.

Once they reached the bay and Emma had regained some composure, Rondie jumped below and grabbed the throwaway phone she kept on her boat for emergencies.

"I've called some agents I know, and they've all said the murders around DC today are related. From what they *didn't* say, the family was killed because they are connected to an extremely sensitive case. There are some very serious players working for the government who want to keep the details of that case highly classified."

Rondie paused and bit her lip. "The other players are willing to kill for the same information. Your dad is either caught in the middle or on one of those sides."

Emma wiped back tears with shaking hands and sniffled. "H-how do you know?"

Rondie brushed her sweat-soaked bangs back. "I don't *know* anything. But my friends gave me a description of the agent who was sent to collect a family from a boat here at this marina. That description matched the guy who was looking for your dad earlier."

"So, you are saying my family is in danger because of Dad's work?"

"That's what I'm guessing."

"Can I call Mom?"

Rondie punched her phone number into the throwaway and held it out to Emma. "Keep it brief and cryptic."

***

An unfamiliar ringtone started playing, and Karen lunged for her bag.

Liam jerked his head toward Karen and barked, "You brought your phone?"

Karen's eyes flew wide, and she frantically scrambled after the phone. "No. It's not mine."

Karen dumped the contents out on the couch and grabbed the phone.

Liam snatched the phone from her hand before she had a chance to answer and shouted, "Don't answer it!" He showed Karen the caller ID. "Do you recognize the number?"

Karen shook her head and leaned back against the couch, disappointed not to see Emma's number. "I borrowed it from a friend. I'm sure it's for her."

Liam glared at Karen. "Why did you bring the phone? Weren't you told to leave it?"

Karen threw up her hands in defeat. "I told you it's not my phone. I was going to use it to call my daughter."

Liam pulled the battery from Rondie's phone and set it on the counter.

Karen lashed back defiantly, "What are you doing? That is the only way my daughter has to get a hold of me!"

Liam ignored her and fished his phone from his pocket then dialed the number that was calling.

Rondie stared at the blocked ID and answered on the second ring. "Hello?" *Silence.* "Hello?" *Click.*

Liam ended the call. "Female. Maybe late fifties?"

Karen shrugged and folded her arms. "Like I said, it's not my phone. It could be anyone." She cocked her brow and asked, "I thought you said you didn't want your phone tracked?"

Liam pursed his lips and gave Karen a contemplative stare. "Mine is a secure phone with special features. I blocked the number. But it's different if your daughter's phone is already hacked. I have designated times I'm to call and check in. I'll check on Emma next time I call in."

He pulled a printed copy of an online magazine from his bag and tossed it at Karen. "This is an online magazine printed by ISIL. Look at page forty-five."

Karen read the title "Assassination Operations". The first article listed an assassination list with some of America's most prominent names and detailed a step-by-step "how to" process for how to assassinate them and other wealthy American entrepreneurs and company owners. The article described targeting these economic personalities to destabilize the American economy and end America's supremacy.

Karen looked up at Liam with a knot in her stomach. "What has this got to do with Bill?"

"This counterterrorism case involves very serious players on both sides. And the players on the good guy's side are starting to disappear. Now turn to page sixty-two."

Karen read through another assassination list detailing members of Congress voting against the nuclear deal. It showed a picture of the U.S. Capitol and discussed methods of infiltrating the building's outer security using silent and assault infiltration. It spelled out a plan specifying targets, based on information they had collected, and told where and when would be the best attack based on security loopholes.

Her hands were shaking when she put the magazine on the couch. "What are you telling me?"

Liam shook his head. "My job is to secure you. But I will say there are only a few people who have access to the undercover names protecting our interests against the pieces of shit who wrote that piece of crap, and two of those families were targeted today— one of which ended in tragic deaths."

Karen stared at Liam through watery eyes. "And Bill is one of those who knows this information?"

Liam put both hands on the wheel and focused straight ahead. He shrugged and repeated, "My job is to secure you."

Karen swallowed the lump in her throat. She checked her watch, 3:15 p.m. *Where are you, Bill?* She stood and started down to the cabin. "I'm going to use the head." She closed the door to the small bathroom and stared at her reflection in the mirror. She pinched the bridge of her nose to stifle an oncoming headache. *What is my next move?*

Chapter 7
Yellow Tape

Monday, May 9th, 2:15 p.m.

Two burly police officers arrived at Emma's house and found the front door half open. Officer Taylor had his gun drawn and called out, "Police." He kept his back against the outside wall and slid his foot along the bottom of the front door to open it. When nothing happened, he ducked into the living room, scoping out the scattered boxes and disarray.

"Check the back. The caller said her boyfriend was stabbed in the alley."

The second officer, Officer Reed, slowly crept through the kitchen with his gun drawn and approached the kitchen door, also left ajar. He cautiously pushed the door with his elbow, opening it wide while he braced his back against the wall and called into the alley, "Police!"

He carefully peeked into the alley, seeing nothing amiss. A coppery smell led him to the garbage bags. Blood was trickling from under the bag and running down the slight incline. Reed pulled a pair of latex gloves from his belt and placed the garbage bags aside.

He saw Blake's nearly decapitated head and knew from past experience he was dead. More sirens screamed toward them through the congested streets while Reed secured the area. A second cruiser blocked the alley, and the officers began marking the crime scene and tagging evidence.

In the next few minutes, the paramedics showed up and eventually loaded Blake's lifeless body into the now-quiet ambulance.

The sirens and ambulance had attracted more curious neighbors, making it increasingly difficult to secure the area. Neighbors were videoing the police activity and snapping selfies with the crime scene in the background.

Officer Taylor stood at the kitchen door and watched the onlookers with disgust before barking orders into the chaos. "Get the tape around the alley and block off the street. Spread out and start interviewing neighbors. Find me someone who has seen or heard something."

He walked through the house and stepped out the front door when a neighbor approached the sidewalk. "What's going on?"

"Police business, ma'am, move along, please."

"Why are they putting all that yellow tape up? I live next door; I deserve to know what is going on."

"Ma'am, please be patient with us. We want your input, but right now we need to secure the crime scene."

"What kind of crime?"

"Ma'am, please." He saw the local news van pull up behind the neighbor.

The officer ignored her question, closed the door to his cruiser and called into the dispatcher. "Yeah, this is Officer Taylor. This is going to turn into a media frenzy. We will need backup on foot immediately."

Officer Reed approached the cruiser with Blake's wallet. "Here is the victim's identification. A neighbor said she saw a young man fitting the victim's description pull up outside the front door. She was upset because he double-parked, blocking her drive."

"Do you have the license plate?"

"Yeah. She wrote it down and was going to call it in if he didn't move it in ten minutes. This establishes a time frame. We put out a BOLO (Be On the LookOut) on the vehicle, and the girl who was seen running out of the house and driving away."

"Do we know who she is?"

"Yeah. Neighbor says her name is Emma Carr. She's a Georgetown student."

Officer Taylor looked up at the suit ducking under the yellow tape and flashing FBI credentials. "Aw, shit. What's he doing here?"

The two officers watched the agent approach with guarded expressions.

A reporter yelled across the yellow tape, "Officer! Do you think this is related to the other family murdered today?"

The agent ignored the reporter's questions and walked toward the cruiser.

The hungry reporter continued with a barrage of questions. "Officer, can you tell us how many bodies were found?"

The FBI agent showed his creds to Officer Taylor. "I'm Agent Stewart. Can I ask you a few questions?"

Taylor squinted up at Stewart and nodded. "Just called for backup."

Stewart arched his brow. "Looks like you'll need it."

Officer Taylor looked over his shoulder at the gathering reporters and motioned for Agent Stewart to follow him into the house.

Once inside, the agent launched into the few facts he knew. "Neighbor isn't far off. This is probably related to the family murdered earlier today. The girl who lives here is the daughter of an Assistant Director. The victim is her boyfriend. I'm guessing an ambush. We've been trying to locate her since this morning. Do you have any idea of her whereabouts?"

Officer Taylor shook his head while he examined the closet door. He pulled the dirty burlap bag from the closet and pulled strands of long hair from the inside of the bag. "She a blonde?"

Officer Reed nodded. "Yes, sir."

Officer Taylor pointed at the fire extinguisher half under the kitchen table. "Looks like the broom and extinguisher were used in a struggle. Let's get some prints."

Agent Stewart crossed his arms and pinched his bottom lip between his thumb and forefinger. "Boyfriend chases suspect out into the alley and meets an armed assailant. Girl gets snatched and locked in closet, but escapes."

Officer Taylor glanced at his watch, 2:35 p.m., and sighed. "That about sums up the preliminaries."

Agent Stewart extended his hand to Officer Taylor. "Thanks for the cooperation. The FBI's focus is finding the girl." He turned and jogged back to his car.

Officer Reed's brows rose with surprise. "That was simple and quick."

Officer Taylor nodded. "Good."

Chapter 8
Briefing

Monday, May 9th, 1:05 p.m.

Monday, May 9th, 1:05 p.m.

By noon, Bill had received word of a report filed from a waitress at The Crab House involving his boat. Two males were fished from the bay after their jet skis were incapacitated by gunshots. The waitress reported the two males as suspicious to her supervisor, and alleged they were chasing the boat. He had not heard any reports about Emma. She had yet to be located, and his calls went straight to her voicemail. His attention was torn between his family and those present around the table.

The Deputy Director paced at the head of the table. "I don't need to tell anyone in this room how serious this is. There are very few with access to this computer system, and even fewer with access to that file. That file contained the names and location of an ongoing op in Syria. Five of the nine names are under cover and have boots on the ground. This tells me there is a mole, and everyone in here will be polygraphed—today. No one leaves the building until every one of you has been questioned.

"I want every camera feed around DC reporting all suspicious activity. All social media traffic is to be monitored. Everyone on the list is a target until we can get ahead of this."

He paused for effect and stared into the eyes of each person in the room. "That OPM (Office of Personnel Management) breach gave them everything they need to know about you and your families."

Everyone nodded nervously. The atmosphere was charged with silent accusations and palpable hostility. The group of Type A personalities stole peripheral glances, silently castigating each other.

The Deputy Director glared at Bill. "Carr!" Bill's whole body snapped to attention. "Do we have an update on a lead?"

"We are following one possible lead. The Alexandria neighbor reported seeing a woman step out the back door wearing a black hoodie, running pants, and shoes, leaving for a run at approximately 5:00 a.m. She assumed it was the neighbor and mother of the small children, and wondered who was watching the kids. She did not see the woman's face, but heard the dog barking when the woman left."

"Anyone else see her running?"

"We are still working that lead."

"Did she see the woman return?"

"No."

"Any leads on the Bethesda murder scene?

"Neighbor reported the fire when she stepped out of the shower closer to 5:30 a.m. But didn't notice anything unusual before that."

"What about leads on the hack?"

"No, sir, but we have slammed shut any chance of further hacks. Codes and passwords have all been changed, and all computers have been scrubbed."

The Deputy Director's face was knotted in a ferocious scowl. He turned to the Agent Davis, the only other agent who had been working directly on the case. "Davis, what about updates on TSLs (Temporary Secure Locations) for the families?"

"They are in motion. We have confirmation from the three other families with boots on the ground. They are living at Ft. Meade and will stay on base. Security has been notified, and extra details will be assigned to those families involved."

The Deputy Director drew a deep breath. "What about Jennings' remaining family?"

"They have been notified. Their locations are scattered, and not considered to be under direct threat. The Bureau has deployed personnel to help them with funeral arrangements."

"Do we have intelligence on whether this is ISIL-inspired or -ordered?"

"No, sir. It appears to have come out of nowhere, similar to the San Bernardino shooters. We didn't have any chatter, cells, or lone wolves hinting at these attacks. We have no known threats against Syrian Op 702 listed under Assistant Director Carr. The hacker group Anonymous appears to be on our side in this one. They shared a lead from their Twitter chatter displaying language and threats that corroborate known FBI intelligence. They are pledging support to help find who is behind these attacks. We also are in contact with the French and Belgian law enforcement agencies, and are comparing names of suspects who may be in the U.S."

Davis continued in clipped sentences. "Other files could have been copied. But they weren't. They went after this sole file. We suspect this is personal to someone. The execution-style killing of the family indicates they are going for revenge."

The group of four debated strategies and speculated about the next target until the Deputy Director marched to the door and turned abruptly to address the table. "I want the results of the polygraphs today; someone in this room leaked classified information. We'll meet back here at 1600 for updates. I want resolution before the end of the day."

Bill checked his watch. 2:15. He glanced up at Jessica. "Have you eaten?"

She shook her head. "No, and I'm starving."

They walked toward the elevator to grab something from the cafeteria. Jessica punched the button and let out a heavy sigh. "Bill, I appreciate you reserving your suspicions about my part in the hack. I promise you my polygraph will alleviate your concerns."

Bill rolled his shoulders to release the tension. "We are the only two people who have logged into that file. One of us has done something to cause this."

Before Jessica could reply, an agent ran toward the elevator. "Sir, I need to speak with you!"

The elevator doors opened, and he waved Jessica to go without him.

"Sir, we have an update on your daughter."

Bill steeled himself for the worst.

"Metro PD issued a BOLO for her. It appears two assailants were waiting for her in her house. She escaped in her boyfriend's car. There were signs of struggle in the house. The boyfriend is dead. We don't have eyes on her, but have tracked her phone to a marina south of Annapolis."

Bill's knees were weak. "She went to our boat." His emotions swung from high to low between pride at Emma's courage and deep grief over the loss of Blake.

"Sir, your wife is on the boat with Agent Garrison. They were last known to be in the bay outside the South River."

Bill ran his hand over his face. "Emma's probably scared senseless, with no place to go."

Someone from down the hall waved at Bill. "Come in here, you need to hear this."

Bill entered a noisy room with large TV screens covering the walls. The agent pointed at the giant TV screen in the middle, showing a reporter on the news reading an online threat from ISIL. A map of the United States was in the background with Maryland, Virginia, Illinois, California and Michigan colored in yellow.

The beauty queen reporter straightened her shoulders and, with a grave face, continued her report. "In an online statement ISIL claims they have seventy trained soldiers in fifteen states, ready at their word to attack any target ISIL desires. Out of seventy trained soldiers, twenty-three have signed up to carry out attacks like the one in DC earlier today.

"A second tragedy in Georgetown involving a young male student is being investigated as another related attack. Neighbors who were interviewed said they spotted the young woman who lives in the house fleeing the scene."

Bill steadied himself against the doorjamb. Out of the corner of his eye, he noticed the other large screen showing the weather channel. He pointed to the screen. "Turn that up."

The weatherman was forecasting heavy storms for the early afternoon and later that night. "Gale winds and coastal flood warnings will wreak havoc with the bay over the next twelve hours."

The weather report triggered Bill's nervous habit to run his hand over his face, and he muttered "*shit*" under his breath. Gritting his teeth, he cursed himself for the unfinished projects he left in the trawler's engine room. He knew if the boat was in rough water, the loosened fittings would leak. He had been in the process of changing several hoses and replacing the dripless seal on the shaft, and had to leave the project only half complete.

"Do we know the boat's location? Can I contact him?"

"I'm sorry, sir. I was told to collect your phone for IT analysis, and you are not to make personal calls. Agent Garrison has call-in check points, and I will relay his progress to you."

Bill was seething inside that his twenty-five years of service to the government were now being viewed with suspicion. But he understood the precautions. He dug his phone from his jacket and handed it to the agent.

The others in the room pretended not to hear the exchange, but the tension had escalated to new highs. Everyone considered Bill beyond reproach. He played strictly by the rules, and went the extra mile to be cautious and fair. If he was under suspicion, then no one was safe.

Bill locked his jaw, turned on his heel, and walked back to his office to resume what he was working on at the computer. The computer had automatically logged him off after five minutes of inactivity. He typed in his password. *Incorrect password* popped up. He realized the cap lock button was on. He unlocked the caps and typed in his password a second time. *Incorrect password.* His level of frustration hit the red zone. He reined in his impatience and examined his password steps. *Was he using the right password?* He noticed the password was over one space. He hit the delete key to start his password in the correct position and started over. *Password incorrect. Too many tries. This account has been locked.*

Bill leaned back and gripped the arms of the chair, cursing under his breath. He waited a full minute to calm down before he called IT to unlock his computer.

After punching a series of numbers to get past the automated troubleshooting, Bill heard a familiar voice answer. "IT."

Bill almost hung up on the arrogant little ass when he heard Jared's voice. The last thing he needed was a smug little millennial trying to prove himself at his expense. He sighed heavily and dropped his forehead in his hand.

***

The IT department was a windowless concrete room containing about a dozen cubicles, and lots of computers, hardware, and spare parts. Jared was the only one of the dozen or so other IT guys who was employed by an outside contractor. The others all worked directly for the FBI. He had hired on a year ago, hoping to get a full-time position with the FBI. He considered himself the smartest of the IT guys, and by far the fastest troubleshooter. He was quick to jump at opportunities to fix the more complicated IT problems, and first to tell the others how to do their jobs. It irritated him when the white-hairs called him for mundane questions and jobs, especially when they were basically too old to remember their own passwords.

When he got the call from Bill to unlock his computer, he rolled his eyes, irritated because he wanted to go on break. Instead of wasting his time going up to Bill's office, he asked if he could take control of his computer from the IT room. Bill gave his permission, and within a few keystrokes, Bill was back online.

Jared smiled patronizingly into the phone and mouthed the required pleasantries before hanging up and shuffling into the cafeteria for his break, joining a round table with a diverse group of coworkers from other departments.

Jessica checked her watch, 2:30 p.m. She approached the counter and opened her mouth to place her order.

The older woman behind the counter smiled and interrupted her. "Reuben sandwich on rye with extra Swiss."

Jessica smiled and turned up her palms. "I like a good Reuben."

She was passing by Jared's table when a coworker called her over to ask if she planned to play on their softball team. While discussing the team and schedules, she couldn't help but overhear Jared bragging about his hot girlfriend. Jessica sneaked a peek at the picture he was showing around the table on his phone.

She walked away wondering how an arrogant little zit-faced IT nerd had landed *that* girl. She took a bite of her Reuben sandwich and headed back upstairs. *Probably not even his girlfriend.*

Jessica finished her sandwich and tossed the wrapper into the garbage while waiting for the elevator. When the elevator doors opened, her phone chimed with a text saying her polygraph was scheduled for 3:30 p.m.

Chapter 9
Storm Clouds

Monday, May 9th, 3:30 p.m.

Karen's stomach growled as she came up from the cabin's head. "You hungry?"

Liam nodded. "Starving."

Karen walked through the salon and down into the galley to hunt through the refrigerator and cabinets for something to eat. "Can we pull into a marina for lunch?"

Liam shook his head. "Negative. We need to keep moving to reach our TSL." When he saw her frown, he added, "Temporary Secure Location." He craned his neck to look up at the clouds through the windshield. "Winds are kicking up. It's supposed to storm."

"Well, we have our choice of peanut butter and jelly on crackers, protein bars, or oatmeal packets. There are also chips and pretzels in the bar, along with a wide variety of booze."

Liam had the kind of smile that lit up a room with charm. "I'd like to say I'll have a beer and pretzels, but I've gotta drive."

Karen pulled out a bottle of vodka and mixed a drink at the bar. "My nerves could use one." She opened the little bar freezer for ice. "Jackpot! We've got a pizza." She brushed the frost off of it. "I'm not sure how old it is, though."

Karen carried her drink and went back to the galley to start the oven.

"I'll take a protein bar while the pizza cooks."

Karen tossed a granola bar up to him and set the oven temp to 400°. She joined him in the salon, enjoying a slight buzz from the liquor on an empty stomach. "I found cookies in the bottom drawer along with some tortilla chips and salsa. Another water?"

"Sure."

Karen climbed back down to the galley and opened the refrigerator door when a wave slammed against the side, causing the boat to pitch and the refrigerator door to slam against the doorjamb behind it. Condiments fell from the racks, and bottles of water tumbled from the fridge. "What's going on?"

Liam's brows knit together. "Wind and waves have picked up. Storm is coming in faster than I expected."

Karen scooped up the clutter on the floor, returned everything to the fridge, and shut the door, double-checking the latch. When she looked back, she saw that the pillows on the outside deck furniture were blown off and teetering next to the rails. Using the teak handholds, she climbed up to the outside deck to rescue her cushions and pillows, tossing them into the salon and securing the loose furniture with bungee cords.

Liam glanced over his shoulder. "Everything good?"

"I'm going to run up to the fly bridge and zip down the windows in the bridge enclosure before it starts to rain." She stepped out from the salon to the outside deck, then up the ladder to the bridge.

Karen's hair was sticking out in all directions when she slid the heavy door shut on the salon. "Whew! It's really windy. We need to dock somewhere."

Liam shook his head. "It's only about ten knots. This boat will handle thirty to forty knots. What's it draw?"

Karen raised a brow. "Three and a half. Why?"

"So I can to keep us out of shallow water."

The oven buzzer was sounding, so Karen went to check the pizza. She opened the oven door, but the pizza wasn't cooked. She looked at the timer on the stove and saw it still had ten more minutes. The buzzer was still going.

She felt a chill of foreboding. "That wasn't the pizza buzzer."

Liam looked down at the control panel and saw the red light on the bilge alarm flashing. "Well, that isn't good. It's the bilge alarm. Where's the engine access?"

Karen pulled back the rug on the floor to expose the hatch to the engine room.

"I can't let go of this wheel. Go down there and see what is going on."

Karen picked up the hatch and set it aside. The minute she climbed down the stairs, she heard the rushing water. There was water rising over the slatted catwalk from the bottom of the boat. She placed her hands and feet cautiously while she waded across the narrow catwalk between the two huge engines, barely avoiding the moving belts and gears while the boat tossed and rocked. She bent down at the end of the catwalk and saw the unfinished project Bill had been working on.

She yelled up at Liam, "The seal on the propeller shaft failed. Water is pouring in." She only knew this because she remembered sitting in the engine room handing Bill tools while he loosened all the clamps around seal. The new dripless seal was still in the trunk of his car.

She waded over and grabbed the orange five-gallon bucket and started bailing.

When the bucket was full, she yelled up at Liam. "I can't lift this. You are going to have to dump this bucket so I can keep filling it."

Liam reached down with one hand while keeping the other securely on the wheel. "If you can lift it to the second stair, then I can reach it from there."

Karen heaved the heavy bucket up to the second stair while the boat pitched, splashing her with water from the bucket and breaking her fingernail. "Dammit!"

The roped muscles in Liam's arm flexed and bulged while he lifted the water. "Climb up here and take the helm while I dump this over the side."

Karen took the wheel and motioned at the side window. "You can slide open that side window and dump it if you don't want to carry it outside. It'll be quicker."

Karen handed back the wheel to Liam, grabbed the empty bucket, and went below again and again until she could barely lift her arms, and her calf and thigh muscles were cramping from the squatting and bending.

After more than twenty buckets, Liam screamed over the buzzer, "This isn't working. The pumps can't keep up with the leak."

Karen yelled back, "I need something to stop the flow." Her internal light bulb went off, and she caught a second wind. She raced up the ladder to the bathroom in their bedroom.

"What are you doing?" Liam screamed from the helm. "Take this wheel. I'll go down there."

"No! I've got this!" She ran back with a box of sanitary napkins they kept in the medicine cabinet in case of a severe cut.

Liam looked at her like she'd grown a new head. "What the hell are you doing?"

The pizza buzzer was screaming along with the bilge alarm. She dropped the box of pads on the counter and pulled the pizza from the oven, then grabbed the duct tape from the shelf and jumped down through the open hatch. She dropped to her knees and crawled instead of walking to the back of the engine room, so she could avoid the moving belts, and opened the box of pads.

She yelled back up to Liam, "Shut off the left engine! I can't work on a turning shaft."

Liam shut down the left engine, and the boat slowed to three knots.

Karen wrapped duct tape around the seal, then strapped a pad around the tape, then wrapped a plastic bag over it with more duct tape.

The water slowed. "It worked!"

Once the water was down to a manageable level and the bilge alarm stopped, Karen crawled up the ladder. "The pumps will hold as long as the duct tape does, but we need to dock this boat soon."

Lightning flashed in the west, and a clap of thunder pounded in the background, emphasizing her point.

Liam examined the radar display to chart a course away from the storm. "If we go north we'll get out of the storm. We're approaching the Bay Bridge, so we should be able to find somewhere on the Eastern Shore once we get past the bridge. It shouldn't be long."

"Bill uses a mechanic out of Rock Hall, and they have a nice marina."

Liam restarted the left engine and headed north. *Buzzzzz.* He smacked his hand against the bilge gauge. "Your fix isn't gonna last; we'll duck into Kentmoor."

Karen watched the Thomas Point Lighthouse fade from sight and dropped into the cushioned booth across from the galley to cut the pizza. Every cell in her body was exhausted. The adrenaline rush from the last half hour of bailing water, along with fears for Emma and the drama from the morning left her almost comatose. She handed Liam three slices of pizza on a paper plate before sinking into the cushion and staring into space while eating her pizza.

Liam leaned down to the galley table to where Karen sat. "You okay?"

Karen barely had the strength to answer. She glared at him and said, "Livin' the dream." She fell back against the cushion and closed her eyes. Her wet hair was stuck to her head, and her wet clothes were clinging uncomfortably and chafing in unmentionable areas.

Exhaustion was weighting Karen's eyelids when she heard Liam talking softly on his phone.

"I don't think she knows anything." *Pause*.

Karen's ears perked up while she listened, feigning sleep.

"We may have to do something else." *Pause*. "You need to do it. It's the only way."

Chapter 10
Tased

Monday, May 9th, 3:30 p.m.

The winds had kicked up past twenty knots before they reached the bay, and Rondie regretted her decision to leave the river. Waves, wind, and a crosscurrent were pitching the thirty-six-foot sailboat from side to side. She dropped the mainsail and turned the boat around to motor back, barking orders for Emma to steer directly toward the red buoy at the mouth of the river while she hustled to secure the sail.

"We're going to head back to the marina. Stay below. No one knows you are here."

Two minutes passed, and Emma popped back up on deck. "I'm going to be sick if I stay down there. I need the fresh air."

Lightning flashed and rain started pelting them. Rondie pointed at the vinyl windshield. "Unsnap those straps and extend that dodger!"

Emma's hands were shaking when she pulled on the little straps, releasing the folded dodger. She stretched the metal ribbed canvas back, creating a roofed enclosure for the wheel.

"Good! Now, unzip that canvas on the back and connect the rear dodger with the front by zipping it shut."

Emma struggled against the wind to unzip the canvas and fasten it to the front. It kept slipping from her fingers and flapping in the wind. When she finally was able to connect the zipper, the enclosure zipped shut, protecting them from the storm.

Rondie craned her neck to see around the blind spots created by the canvas. The wind blasted against the canvas loudly while they motored back down the river. Thankfully, the waves weren't as high as in the bay.

When she was close to the marina where she docked her boat, she spotted the police. "There are uniformed police on the pier interviewing people. We can't dock here. We're going across the cove, over to The Tiki Bar and Restaurant, where we can watch things play out."

Emma nodded and chewed her thumbnail.

Rondie motored past the pier and the moored boats down to the Tiki Bar. Several other boats were tied up at the Tiki Bar's pier to ride out the storm. She reached inside the cabin and grabbed her raincoat, shrugging into it while she steered the boat to the opposite side of the bar and tucked in between two larger boats for cover.

Rondie unzipped the enclosure and glanced over her shoulder at Emma, who was rain-soaked and shivering. "Stay here. I'm going to secure the lines. You hungry? I can grab a couple burgers."

Emma bit her upper lip and nodded. "Thanks."

Rondie pointed inside the cabin. "There are some towels under the bench seats in the galley you can use to get dried off."

A young dock boy appeared on the pier in rain gear, and Rondie threw him one of the lines. She jumped off her boat and secured the other lines, then disappeared inside the bar.

The country music playing in the background added to the upbeat atmosphere in the bar, a stark contrast to the mood on her boat. The levity of the crowded bar was a welcome respite. She felt sorry for Emma, but was regretting her involvement. She had started her day with a to-do list for her boat. Not one item was crossed off, and she was suffering through teenaged melodrama besides. She wasn't sure what was true regarding the boyfriend and his car. Did Emma steal it? Her story was pretty far-fetched.

Rondie took a seat at the bar and listened to the TV in the upper corner. The weatherman was standing in front of a map showing the Annapolis area covered in red and orange.

She ordered two burgers and a beer from the bartender and listened to the other boaters at the bar embellish boat tales, increasing the drama with every beer they consumed.

"Breaking News" flashed across the screen, and a young woman in a yellow slicker standing in front of a yellow crime tape appeared on the screen. "DC is in a state of shock while police are going door-to-door, interviewing neighbors for any information in the two separate homicides. I'm standing in front of the latest victim's house. A young male reported to be a Georgetown student was found brutally slain in the alley behind this house a little more than an hour ago. Police are saying very little, but a neighbor told me she saw the female student who lives here, Emma Carr, fleeing in the boyfriend's car. A BOLO for her was issued, and police have found the car parked at a marina south of Annapolis. Someone from the marina reported her family docked their boat there, and the mother was seen leaving the slip earlier today."

Rondie was listening so intently to the television she didn't hear the bartender until he shook the brown bag with hamburgers in her face.

"Order's up!"

Rondie paid her bill and slowly finished her beer until the newscast broke for commercial.

***

Emma spied the throwaway phone on the galley table and scrolled through the list to redial the number Rondie had dialed earlier. *Nothing.* Just an automated voice telling her the person at the number was unavailable.

She wrapped the towel tighter and closed her eyes, trying to process the morning events. It was impossible to believe that a few short hours ago her biggest problem was avoiding her parents long enough to party with her friends. Tears rolled down her cheeks when she thought about the calls she had ignored. *What would have happened if she'd answered? Were those the last calls she'd ever get from her parents? And what about Blake? Was he going to be all right?* She shivered when she remembered the blood dripping from the long knife and the look of vicious satisfaction on the guy's face when he said the problem was solved.

Emma's thoughts were interrupted by the sound of someone boarding the boat. She glanced out the porthole and saw Rondie tugging the line closer to the finger dock so she could climb on deck.

Emma wiped at her eyes and took a long, slow breath to hide her tears.

Rondie handed the greasy brown sack to Emma and eased out of the wet raincoat. She stepped down into the cabin and grabbed some paper plates from the shelf over the table, then reached over to the small fridge. "Want a bottled water or soda?"

Emma's voiced cracked. "Thanks, a water would be great."

Rondie settled on the cushion across the booth from Emma and divvied up the burgers while she gathered her thoughts. "Well, the news was on."

Emma stared at Rondie with wide eyes and a mouth full of burger. She reached for one of the napkins stuffed in a plastic holder on the little table.

Rondie raised her left brow. "The police have a BOLO out on you."

Emma pinched her brows in a worried fret. "What's that?"

"Be On the LookOut." She exhaled and leaned back against the booth. "You need to turn yourself into the police and explain what happened."

Emma's shrill whine scraped at Rondie's nerves. "I tried calling them earlier to tell them, but my phone died, and then you told me to ditch it, and everything has just been so confusing. I thought I'd just get Mom and Dad to come with me and sort all this out. Did the news mention Blake?"

Rondie swallowed her bite of burger and took a sip of water. "He was murdered."

Emma's voice rose to dog whistle pitch. "He's dead?"

Rondie nodded her head solemnly. "I'm sorry."

"I knew it. I…I knew it." She exhaled loudly. "I knew it when I saw that knife. Those animals!" She dropped her face in her hands and sobbed.

Rondie picked at her burger while Emma cried it out. After Emma regained a bit of her composure, Rondie cleared her throat and said, "We need to contact the police."

"What will happen to me? I need to talk to Mom and Dad. *Where are they?*"

"I don't know, but at this point, I'm harboring a fugitive. Let's finish our burgers and pull back into my slip so we can talk to one of the officers."

"What are we going to say?"

"I'm going to tell them we went to find your mom, and the storm got bad, so we turned around. And you are going to tell them the truth. You were fleeing from some really bad men and were running to your parents."

Emma's voice was frail and her eyes were pleading. "If they take me to jail, will you go with me?"

Guilt plagued Rondie, because, in truth, what she really wanted was to go home to her peaceful house and be done with this. She knew if she followed through with the police, this would only be the beginning of her involvement.

"Please? I can't do this by myself."

Rondie patted Emma's hand. "Sure, sure no problem. I'm sure they'll want both our stories."

Before they left the pier, Rondie had a sinking feeling about the police across the cove at the marina. She called her friend at the FBI to discuss how they should handle the situation with Emma. He agreed to pass on their location to Agent Stewart, who was in charge of collecting Emma.

While she motored away from the Tiki bar, she swung out into the channel to avoid the moored sailboats, but as she grew closer to the pier where her slip was, she noticed two police officers talking at the end of the pier. That was the first thing that struck her as odd. Why would they be standing clear at the end of the pier in the rain?

Rondie poked her head into the cabin and called to Emma. "Hand me those binoculars from that hook over the galley, would ya?"

She shifted into neutral and tried to maintain her position against the wind so she could get a closer look at the uniformed police. Things weren't adding up. One had on running shoes with black pants and white button-down shirt. The police jacket and hat appeared authentic but ill fitting. But the real giveaway was his duty belt. It was a wide brown leather belt with a cell phone case, empty gun holster, and a knife slipped through a loop that would normally house a baton.

Rondie let go of the breath she was holding to keep the binoculars still and sighed. "Houston, we have a problem."

Emma stood at the bottom of the cabin stairs looking up at Rondie. "What's the matter?"

"Uniforms don't add up."

She raised the glasses again and examined the other uniform. "Black running shoes, gun tucked into a leather belt, black pants stained with what appeared to be blood—what the f—? Emma, come up here and get a good look at these two. Do these look like the two that were waiting for you in your house?"

Emma couldn't get her feet to move. "I don't want them to see me."

Rondie saw the color drain from Emma's face and her hands start shaking again. She handed her the field glasses. "Here, take these and look out the porthole."

Her hands were shaking so badly she could barely see the two officers on the pier. "I'm just not sure. I didn't get a good look at them. They're around the same age and height, I think."

Rondie called her friend back to check on Agent Stewart's whereabouts. "Hey, what's the ETA on Stewart? We have a problem at the dock. I need a different location."

Her friend agreed to pass on the information to Agent Stewart and have him call Rondie directly.

The storm was now making it harder to avoid the moored boats. She didn't want to create attention by turning the boat around to go back to the Tiki Bar, so she pulled straight past her slip on the pier to the little restaurant at the marina. There were four empty slips at the edge of the marina restaurant. She eased into the one closest to the building as carefully as possible in deference to the heavy winds. A dock boy appeared, and she slipped out of the dodger and threw him the lines.

"Thanks, I'll be a minute," shouted Rondie.

The dock boy gave a dismissive wave and secured her lines to the pilings. "Take your time."

Emma handed the phone to her when she stepped down into the cabin. "Someone just called, but I didn't answer."

Rondie took off her wet coat and ran a towel over face. "They'll call back."

Before she could sit down, the phone rang. Rondie picked up the phone. "Rondie."

"This is Agent Stewart. I was given this number and told you have a package?"

"I do. What is your ETA?"

"We're five minutes from the parking lot. I have backup in a separate car. I understand you have a problem."

"It's your problem now. Two guys at the end of the pier aren't cops. I'm guessing you will find they are the two from the same location my package departed."

"Okay, we'll take care of that. Can you deliver the package to the parking lot?"

"No problem."

"We're in two black Ford SUVs. My plates are Charlie Delta 943."

"Got it."

Rondie reached under the galley tabletop and retrieved the 9mm Luger she kept duct-taped in plastic underneath. She checked the cartridge and slid off the safety from the gun. "I'm going to walk you to the parking lot in a few minutes and hand you off to Agent Stewart with the FBI, who will take you into custody. You will be safe with him. He's going to take you into DC and hand you off to your dad. I'm guessing after that, you will be interviewed and put somewhere safe for a while."

Emma looked at her with pleading eyes. "Can't you go with me?"

Rondie pulled a shoulder holster from over the stove and slipped it on. Rondie checked her watch, 4:30. "Under the present circumstances, it'll be better this way. I'm going to keep an eye on our two friends on the pier until someone gets here, and I'll need to move my boat back to the slip and close it down. By the time all that happens, you'll be with your dad and out of harm's way."

"Okay, you're going to walk me to his car, right?"

Rondie lifted the top of an empty box of detergent, pulled out a taser and handed it to Emma. "Yep. You know how to use this?"

Emma's eyes were the size of quarters when she reached out for the gun. "I'm not sure."

"Nothin' to it." Rondie took it, pulled the safety, and handed it back to Emma. "Just pull the trigger if someone grabs you. It'll drop them immediately."

Emma held the taser cautiously. "Where should I put it?"

"Cross your arms and hold it close to your body, but keep your finger off the trigger. Put this rain poncho on and stay close behind me with your head down."

"Okay."

"You ready?"

Emma put her hand over her stomach. "I'm so scared; I feel like I'm about to throw up."

Rondie's mouth pulled to the side. "You'll be fine. Take a deep breath and shake off the nerves."

Emma took a deep breath and forced her feet to move forward. "Okay, I'm as ready as I'll ever be."

Rondie opened the enclosure and stepped out first. The boat was rocking in the narrow slip, but the pilings gave the two of them something to hang on to while they climbed onto the dock. "Remember, stay close, and keep your head down."

They walked outside on the narrow, side deck to the windowless front of the restaurant. As they walked through the parking lot, they approached the large awning over the front doors. Emma looked up and saw someone she knew talking on his cell phone. At first glance, she felt relief to see someone she knew. But the expression on his face set off a warning signal. He abruptly ended the call, and walked into the restaurant.

Emma's voice sounded like it was coming from someone else. "Hi, Cal."

She heard the sound of feet running behind her before she saw the fake officer running toward her, wielding a ten-inch knife and shouting, "*Allahu akbar!* (God is Great)"

A gunshot echoed after a clap of thunder, and she saw blood spurt from her attacker's knee. Emma was shoved to the ground, and a bolt of pain blasted through her shoulder when she hit the pavement.

She crawled to her knees and heard screeching tires. Rondie was yelling, "Stay down."

In the commotion, the phony officer who'd been shot in the knee fell across Emma's leg. He gripped her calf, and she kicked at him frantically while pulling the trigger on the taser.

Rondie gave him a swift kick to the kidney, and he rolled away from Emma screaming in pain from the two small dart-like electrodes attached to his shoulder. She kicked the knife into the bushes just as Agent Stewart joined them.

Agent Stewart wrapped his beefy arms around Emma's chest from behind and pulled her backward, forcing her into a car. She was kicking, screaming and crying hysterically while the SUV peeled out of the parking lot.

The second fake cop came charging around the corner also yelling *"Allahu akbar,"* whipping his head from side to side searching for Emma. He waved his gun at Rondie, clearly misinterpreting her grey hair. "Where's the girl?"

Rondie glared at him down the barrel of her gun and spoke in a calm, lethal voice. "Put down the gun, or I'll shoot you dead."

The guy grinned dismissively and pointed his gun at her. She dropped him with a clean shot to the shoulder. Then held her gun on him while she kicked his away. "Now, what did I tell you?"

He was writhing in pain, struggling to sit up. "Bitch!"

"I'm trying to be nice. I gave you two a second chance. You could be dead." She'd inflicted more pain than injury on them. She knew the drill. The point was to make them talk.

Three large men dressed in black fatigues climbed out of the second SUV and immediately subdued the two men on the ground. "Hello, Rondie. I thought you were retired."

She smiled. "I see they sent the three stooges for my backup." She gave them a half shrug and cocked her head. "I still like to have a little fun every now and again."

"I can see that. What do we have here?"

She pointed at the two fake cops. "I think these two may need a couple of Band-Aids."

Larry nodded at the other two agents to cuff the suspects on the ground. He looked at the blood pooling under each man. "You may be right."

She had trained the three men down at Quantico and liked to push their buttons. They were good, but cocky. She had dubbed them *The Three Stooges* because one was named Larry, another was nicknamed Mo, short for Monroe, and the other had uncontrollable curly hair.

She nodded toward the front awning. "We have a stray. His name is Cal. Good-looking, with curly black hair. Jeans. Navy blue jacket. I think he slipped inside. Emma greeted him, and he tipped these two off."

Rondie turned and waved at the lead agent. "Larry, you follow me inside, and let Mo and Curly keep these two company."

"Still not funny, Rondie."

A sly grin spread across her face. "It is to me."

Rondie walked through the almost-empty restaurant and spotted Cal near the back door of the bar. "Go around to the back. I'll give you two minutes, and then I'll approach him."

Two minutes passed and Rondie walked through the bar. Cal saw her and pushed open the door, running directly into Larry. Together, they cuffed Cal and walked him to the front of the restaurant.

An ambulance was rounding the corner when Rondie got back to the parking lot.

She pointed to the two guys who had been handcuffed and were still lying on the ground. "So, Cal, do you know these two?"

Cal stared straight ahead. "I want a lawyer."

Chapter 11
Polygraphs

Monday, May 9th, 2:45 p.m.

Bill walked into the small nondescript room and extended his hand to the polygraph examiner. "Bill Carr."

The examiner greeted him pleasantly, shook his hand and introduced herself. "Debbie Smith. Please come in and take a seat in this chair." The chair sat at the side of the desk and faced the blank wall. "I know you have been through this before, but for the record, I need to tell you this exam is being videotaped."

Bill nodded. Polygraphs were required by the Bureau for all employees with a high security clearance. He had been through countless sessions over the years.

Debbie took a seat at an old metal desk with a laptop and a number of tubes and wires laid out. "This exam will take about an hour, so please make yourself comfortable. If you need to take a break or use the restroom, just let me know. If you would like some water, I'll get it for you."

Bill nodded once in acknowledgement.

"Are you taking any medications?"

"No."

"Are you in good health?"

"Yes."

"How much sleep have you had in the last thirty-six hours?"

"Ha. Little to none."

Debbie typed his responses to a long list of mundane questions about his health condition, medications, hospitalizations, background, address, and so on.

"We'll begin by discussing the reason you are here, and you can explain your involvement with the leaked file. We will verify your explanation with a series of yes or no questions once we attach the polygraph."

Bill drew a deep breath and propped an ankle on his knee.

"Let's start with the file. I realize the information in the file is confidential, but let's talk about who had access to it and ways it might have been hacked."

Bill described as much as he could remember about the file, and named Jessica, Agent Davis, the Deputy Director, and himself as the only four who had physical access to the file, since the others listed were undercover in Syria.

Bill and Debbie discussed his theories about the breached file for nearly twenty minutes.

"Anything else you would like to add before I hook you up and verify your answers?"

Bill shook his head. "No, I don't think so."

Debbie came around and attached rubber tubes around his chest and abdomen. "These will record your breathing."

She put a blood pressure cuff around his upper arm. "This may be uncomfortable. It will be inflated for about five minutes at a time and will record changes in blood pressure and pulse."

Bill anticipated the leads and held up his fingers.

Debbie placed the leads on his fingers and explained, "These will record changes in your SNS (Sympathetic Nervous System)."

Bill uncrossed his legs and sat up straight.

"It's very important that you sit straight and very still. The sensors in the pad you are sitting on will record any movement or muscle contractions during the exam."

Bill calmed his mind and concentrated on answering the questions with clarity.

"Is your name Bill Carr?"

"Yes."

"Do you intend to tell the truth?"

"Yes."

"Are you in the Hoover Building?"

"Yes."

"Are you married?"

"Yes."

"Do you have three children?"

"No."

Bill found the verification questions boring, but knew they helped the examiner establish a baseline. After the first series of questions was completed, the pressure cuff was released.

Debbie smiled. "Doin' okay?"

Bill pursed his lips and nodded. After a few minutes, she inflated the cuff and began the next series of questions.

"Have you at any time shared classified information with anyone who doesn't have clearance?"

"No."

"Do you have knowledge of anyone who might have read your files?"

"Yes."

"Is that person Jessica Murphy?"

"Yes."

"Do you think she leaked the material in that file?"

Bill hesitated. "I don't know."

"Do you have suspicions she might have leaked the information in the file?

"Yes."

"Do you suspect Davis leaked the information?"

"No."

The examiner reworded the same question around Jessica a dozen or so more times before the pressure cuff was released again.

Debbie typed a few lines into the laptop and asked. "Need some water or anything?"

Bill shook his head. "No, I'm good." He just wanted the exam over with.

Debbie inflated the cuff again.

"Was there any time that you were away from your computer with this particular file openly displayed on the monitor?

"Not that I recall."

"Did anyone use your desk and access your computer who could read that file?"

"No."

The questions continued for an hour with the cuff inflating and deflating until Bill's arm felt like it was asleep. He was mentally exhausted and wiping sweat from his brow when she asked the final question.

Relief swept over Bill when Debbie released the wires and tubes. She looked over the charts and smiled. "You passed your exam. You are free to go."

Bill stood, stretched and drew a deep breath. "Thank you."

A question was playing at the edge of Bill's subconscious as he stood to leave. He had remembered something during the line of questioning that he wanted to explore. *What was it?*

He walked out of the interview room and saw Jessica sitting in a chair waiting to by polygraphed in the reception room. He checked his watch, 3:30 p.m.

It was something about Jessica. What was it he wanted to remember? He waited for the elevator and mentally went through the list of questions involving Jessica. He stepped into the elevator and punched in his floor, continuing to run through the list of questions. He thought back to the last time he opened the file. Jessica came in while the file was open on his computer to complain there were computer problems, and she was sick of calling IT. His computer froze while she was standing there. That was it. *But what did that mean?*

* * *

Jessica sat in the same chair Bill had occupied thirty minutes earlier. She was taking slow breaths to calm her nerves. She checked the time. 4:00 p.m.

She was asked the usual list of questions about her medications, health, hospitalizations, background, address, what kind of work she did, how much sleep she'd had, and a litany of other basic inquiries.

Her polygraph followed the same protocol as Bill's. They began with basic profile questions, then Jessica was given the opportunity to discuss everything she knew about the case, which they would then verify with the polygraph.

Her polygrapher, Debbie, took a sip of her water. "You sure you don't want some water?"

Jessica's mouth was dry. "Well, okay."

Debbie handed her a small bottle of water. "Let's start with why you logged into the file last week."

Jessica took a sip. "It was just routine. I was updating stats from data I'd received."

"Have you discussed the stats or any of the contents of the file with anyone else?"

Jessica's stomach flipped, and she inhaled a deep breath, exhaling slowly to form her words carefully. "I have not discussed the op with anyone, but I have discussed the leak with my boyfriend."

Debbie jotted something on her notepad. "Who is your boyfriend?"

Jessica winced. "That's the other thing…Liam Garrison is the agent sent to collect Bill's wife."

"Liam is your boyfriend?"

Jessica nodded.

"Let's go back to what you told him about the file."

"Two days ago when the threat came in, I told Liam someone had accessed a classified file about a Syrian operation and were threatening to kill everyone named in the file. We talked about whether it was a bluff and if it was possible that someone had simply gotten lucky guessing the name of the op."

"Did you discuss the names on the cover sheet with Liam?"

"Not until I knew they had been leaked. We were just bouncing different scenarios about how that file could have been hacked, since Bill and I are the only ones with authorized access to the file." Jessica threw her hands up. "And I know it wasn't me who leaked it."

"How long have you been involved with Liam?"

Jessica's eyes softened. "We met when I was working in the DC field office about three and a half years ago. I thought he was an arrogant ass—a gorgeous one, but still an ass. It wasn't until we were working undercover in a van at night for a week that we started seeing each other. After that, our supervisor found out and gave the ultimatum that one of us had to move on.

"Relationships are tough with this job. Liam and I understand each other. I knew the gossip would impugn my professional image if I stayed, so when the opportunity to be Bill Carr's Special Assistant opened shortly thereafter, I interviewed and got the job. Liam and I have been together ever since, but agreed to keep it quiet so it wouldn't interfere with our careers. It's not that we hide it; we just don't make it public.

Jessica found herself sharing more with Debbie than she intended to. She was easy to talk to, and created a safe environment.

She also explained that she had called Liam earlier today to see if Bill had talked to his wife, Karen, about the leaked file. She knew this would lead to more conflict later.

After an hour of discussing the case, Debbie raised her brows. "Do you have anything else you want to discuss before we verify your answers?"

"I don't think so. I'm ready."

Debbie smiled and gave her spiel about the wires and leads while she attached them to Jessica. She inflated the cuff and began the questions.

They began with the basic list of mundane profile questions to establish a baseline. After the first series of questions were finished the cuff was released, and Debbie checked the charts.

"Doin' okay? Need anything?"

Jessica shook her head, anxious to continue. Once again, the cuff was inflated.

"Have you ever shared classified information with anyone without clearance?"

"No."

"Have you ever discussed the information in the leaked file with anyone other than Bill Carr?"

"Yes."

"Is that person listed on the cover sheet of that file?"

She drew a deep breath. "No."

Jessica squirmed in her seat, and the seat sensors started registering her nervousness.

Debbie reminded Jessica to remain still.

Jessica knew she was in trouble for discussing the file, but it would be worse if she lied about it.

"Is Liam Garrison the only person you discussed the file with other than Assistant Director Bill Carr?"

Jessica cleared her throat. "Yes."

"Does Liam Garrison have a security clearance?"

"Yes."

"Are you in a romantic relationship with Liam Garrison?"

A blush crept up Jessica's neck to her face. "Yes." Why did answering that question make her feel like she was in junior high?

"Has this relationship continued for three and a half years?"

"Yes."

"Have you discussed the operation within that file with Liam Garrison?"

"No."

"Did you share the names involved in that file with Liam Garrison?"

Jessica shifted, setting off the sensors in the seat again. "Yes."

"Did you share information with the intent to harm?"

"No."

The next half hour's worth of questions dug into every facet of what she had shared and why.

"Did you talk to Liam Garrison today?"

Jessica closed her eyes. "Yes."

"Did you make the phone call?"

"Yes."

"Did you discuss the case when you called him?"

"No."

"Did you call Liam Garrison with the explicit reason to ask if Bill Carr's wife knew anything about the case?"

"Yes." Jessica knew husbands talked to wives, and had hoped that Karen would say something to incriminate Bill.

"Did he give you any information you feel would clear your name?"

"No."

Jessica felt suffocated after an hour and a half of a constant barrage of questions. The level of truth extracted left her feeling raw. Every detail of her life felt under scrutiny. She was completely forthright, knowing if she lied it was grounds to be fired.

Debbie unhooked Jessica from the tubes and leads. She examined her charts and smiled politely. "I don't see any problems. You are free to go."

Jessica rubbed her arm where the cuff had been and stretched. Relief poured over her like a cool breeze. She smiled back at Debbie and thanked her before walking out the door.

She checked the time, 5:30 p.m. and turned to see who was calling her name down the hall.

"Jessica, come in here. I think we've got something." The agents who were working the tip line for information regarding the three earlier murders were poring over leads.

"A photo was posted on Twitter a few minutes ago. It's from this morning in Alexandria. Look. It's a person leaving a backpack near the bushes next to the driveway at the Campbell's house earlier today. We've matched that with a security camera from across the street. Now, watch the bag."

She watched as a person in a black jacket stepped off the sidewalk, stuffed the bag into the bushes, then walked to the back of the house.

Jessica leaned into the computer. "That's a female. Zoom in. Look at her hand and the way she shrugs that shoulder strap like it's a purse. I know those pants. They are expensive, and she also has long, blond hair. Zoom in here. That's a hairclip sticking out from the left side of her hood."

"Here's the clip of the bag being retrieved." A woman in a tight black hoodie, spandex running pants and running shoes picked the bag from the bushes and jogged down the walk.

An analyst called from the other side of the room, "Just got a facial shot, and they're feeding it into the facial recognition system now."

Jessica looked closely at the grainy picture. Something was familiar about the girl. "Does Lt. Campbell know about the break-in or targeted threats yet?"

"I don't know. I think they are working on getting him out of Syria since his cover is blown, and they'll probably tell him once he's out and safe."

"What do you think is in the bag?"

"Don't know. Could be anything. We got confirmation the Jennings family was shot before the house was torched."

Another report came in while she was standing there.

"More footage. This one is from the Bethesda attack. Neighbor just emailed this clip from a personal security camera." The room exploded with chatter and chaos. They gathered around their monitors and watched while a figure in a ball cap, dark sunglasses, and jeans grabbed a bag from the bushes, put a piece of paper under a rock, and casually strolled down the sidewalk.

Jessica stared at the screen. "Are they walking away from the house?"

"Yeah. The time stamp says 5:30. That would indicate it was close to the same time as the attempted break-in at the Campbell house."

"That means these were supposed to be simultaneous attacks."

Someone called from another computer. "Same MO as earlier." A large computer screen in the front of the room zoomed in on the shot of bag.

"Can you zoom in on the partially open zipper?"

The camera zoomed in on what looked like a white pipe.

A large man with an earpiece and ill-fitting suit appeared from the hall. "Agent Murphy? You are expected in the Assistant Director's office now."

Jessica read the look on his face. There would be no delaying her departure. She followed him to Bill's office. The serious climate was confirmed when his secretary wouldn't look her in the eye. She just waved her in and said, "The Assistant Director is expecting you."

Jessica walked in with her patented innocent expression.

Bill gave her a steely stare. "Close the door."

Jessica drew in a deep breath while she turned to close the door.

Bill leaned back in his chair and rolled the pen between his fingers. "I don't care what your polygraph said. I think you are complicit in this."

He stood and kicked the garbage can across the room, scattering papers all over the floor. "When were you going to tell me you are *involved* with the agent who has my wife? What's your plan? Is this about money? Where is he taking my wife?"

"Bill! You are being ridiculous! I had no say in which agent they sent to collect Karen. It just happened to be Liam. Call his supervisor. Ask him why he sent Liam. Go on! Call him! Liam knows the back rivers and bay like no one else. He was the most qualified."

"You called him today."

"I did."

"Why?"

Jessica narrowed her eyes with fury. "Because maybe I don't trust *you*. You were right. We are the only two who could have leaked that cover sheet. And I know it wasn't me. I'll admit it; I asked Liam to fish around for information from Karen. I wanted to know if you told her anything about the case."

They locked their eyes in a stare-down.

Bill snarled. "You were in my office the last time I had that file open. You told me we were experiencing technical difficulties, and IT was working on the system. My computer froze while you were standing right there."

"Oh, for Christ's sake, Bill! These computers freeze all the time! They are pieces of shit! Are you seriously going to blame that on me?"

"I know there is something you are not telling me. Who else is involved in this?"

Before Jessica could answer, Bill's secretary knocked and opened the door. "Sir, your daughter is out here."

Emma burst through the door and hurled herself at him. They threw their arms around each other while Emma sobbed, "Daaad! Where's Mom? Blake is dead." She crumpled into uncontrollable sobs while the others quietly left the room.

Chapter 12
Sinking

Monday, May 9th, 4:00 p.m.

Liam shouted down into the galley at Karen from the cabin's helm. "That water sounds worse than it was before. Better go down and check it out."

Karen was close to giving up. Total exhaustion was weighing on her every muscle. It took all her strength to push herself off the cushion and climb the couple of stairs back up to the salon where Liam was at the wheel. She stared down the open hatch into the engine room and climbed down the ladder.

Water was pouring in again, faster than before. The box of pads had fallen over, and was floating all around her. She shook her head at the surreal scene. "How close to shore are we?"

"Close. Why? How bad is it?"

"Bad. If we can't get to shore in less than five minutes, then we need to call for a tow or the coast guard."

Liam checked the gauges in front of the wheel and squinted through the pelting rain, cursing under his breath. "Can you bail 'til we get there?"

Karen looked at the rushing water and got mad at Bill for creating the problem. She wanted to cry but was too tired. The blisters on her fingers throbbed as she picked up the orange bucket and started bailing. The burn in her shoulders and arms was almost unbearable as she heaved the bucket to the first step, then up to the second stair. "I can't do this anymore. I just can't."

Liam reached down and lifted the bucket, dumping it out the side window. "It's okay. We're closer than I thought. I'm almost to the marina, and I see a pump-out station on the gas dock at the end of the pier. I'm going to stop there and use it to bail us out. The leak should slow down once we stop moving."

Karen leaned her head on the top rung of the ladder with relief.

Liam yelled down, "Can you manage the lines?"

Karen closed her eyes and hissed, "I hate this boat!"

Liam coasted the rocking boat along the pilings in front of the pump-out station. "Never mind, they've got a dock boy." Liam hurried up on deck and threw the lines to the kid, quickly explaining that the boat was taking on water and he wanted to use the pump-out to drain it.

The dock boy hunched under his plastic poncho to avoid the pelting rain and unhooked the rolled pump-out tubing. He fed the long, flexible tubing through the side window to Karen at the wheel. She wrinkled her nose and grabbed a paper towel to guide it down into the engine room.

Liam reentered the cabin and grabbed a dishtowel to wipe the rain from his face. He glanced over at Karen and yelled, "Shut off the engines," before he scurried down the engine room ladder to assess the situation. The water level was within an inch of flooding the engines.

He yelled back at Karen. "Tell the dock boy to start the pump!"

Liam crawled to the back of the engine room to reposition the duct tape around the shaft. He bit into the roll of tape, ripping new pieces for the seal. The water had slowed some since the boat was docked. He squinted at the white blobs floating around him, scooping one up to examine it and quickly throwing it across the engine room.

He heard a loud laugh overhead and glanced up to see Karen looking down, laughing at him.

Liam wiped the sweat from his brow with a forearm. "Something funny?"

"You should see the disgusted look on your face!"

"Go see if the dockmaster is here and can pull this boat so we can keep these engines from flooding. Otherwise, I'll move it over to a shallow slip and let it settle on the keel, but it would save the engines if we can have it pulled."

Karen had always dreaded boatyards—too much testosterone. She pulled at her soaked T-shirt and shorts, and growled her annoyance. They were soaked and transparent, of course. She opened the little closet and yanked out Bill's rain slicker, slipping into it quickly. She checked her watch. 5:30 p.m. "I'll be right back."

She gripped the railing with both hands and timed her footing while the boat continued to pitch against the dock. She jumped onto the pier and slid on the wet wood, falling to her knees. Her entire body ached, but she was relieved to be on land. She darted into the restaurant to inquire about the dockmaster.

A young, long-legged waitress chomped her gum and pointed at Karen's knees. "Ma'am, you don't look so good."

Karen bent over, following the pointed finger and saw chunks of splinters sticking out of her knees and blood streaming down her legs. She went from wet and cold to hot and clammy in two seconds. Nausea gripped her when she tried to straighten up, and her surroundings faded to black. The waitress's voice sounded like it was coming from the other end of a long tunnel.

Chapter 13
Tensions Build

Monday, May 9th, 6:15 p.m.

Bill's secretary politely waited until she heard Bill and his daughter talking in normal voices before she interrupted them. "I'm sorry, sir. The Special Agent in charge wants Emma to be interviewed as soon as possible. They are waiting for her at the Washington field office, on the fourth floor in the conference room. There is a car waiting for her down in the garage. You also have a meeting with the Deputy Director in fifteen minutes. Can I get you something from the cafeteria?"

"Thank you, Ellen. I'd appreciate a sandwich. Emma, what about you?"

Emma cleared her throat and straightened her shoulders, attempting to bolster her frail appearance, but her red, swollen eyes and raw voice betrayed her attempted bravado. "No, Dad. I'm not hungry. Rondie and I ate on her boat."

Bill smiled warmly at his secretary. "I'll walk Emma down to the garage."

"Yes, sir. I'll get you a sandwich from the cafeteria, then."

It was arranged that Emma would be brought back to the Hoover Building after her interview.

Bill gave his daughter a hug. "Emma, I'm sorry you got sucked into all this, but I'm so proud of the way you're handling yourself. Just tough it out a little longer. Everything is going to be okay."

He closed Emma's car door and went back to his office. After taking a few seconds to appreciate the quiet, he ate the sandwich his secretary had left for him and contemplated what he should do about Jessica.

He was exhausted. He leaned his head back and closed his eyes to consider his next move.

"Sir, you are due in the Deputy Director's office."

"Thank you, Ellen."

***

Jessica was already seated in the conference room at 6:30 p.m. when Bill arrived. He took the seat opposite her and waited in silence for the Deputy Director. They stood when the DD arrived and exchanged greetings.

The Deputy Director dropped a file on the table and motioned for Bill and Jessica to sit. "Everyone on the cover sheet of the file has passed the polygraph. We know there was no intentional leak from those listed, so now we are focusing on peripheral leaks. Second-level investigations have begun. Anyone who could possibly have come into contact with information about the file will be interviewed."

Jessica and Bill nodded and listened to the DD, ignoring each other.

He glanced from Bill to Jessica and heaved a heavy sigh. "Do you have any updates on today's attacks or any leads on suspects?"

Bill deferred to Jessica with a gesture for her to give the briefing.

Jessica straightened. "Preliminary analysis of information picked up from Data Miner was shared with Brussels and Paris, and they are running it through their intelligence agencies. No credible leads have surfaced. Since the two incidents this morning were simultaneous, we have ruled out a lone wolf in favor of a network. We suspect this network is operating as a separate compartment, and likely has no communication with possible other cells with the same goals.

"Along with the chatter from Data Miner, we are running facial recognition on the female who dropped off the backpack in the Alexandria footage we retrieved earlier today. We are also running a male's photo from a security camera at the Bethesda attack. However, he wore dark glasses and a ball cap covering most of his face. If we can confirm facial recognition, then we will be able to put together a solid lead.

"There are three different females listed on terrorist watch lists since the California attacks that have been traced from Syria. Brussels also identified the three females as having been in a Brussels café outside the airport when the bomb detonated. We suspect that if our female is one of them, then she made her way into the United States from Canada.

"We have a grainy picture of a female from security footage following the first attack in Alexandria, walking down a sidewalk. All cameras have been programmed around DC to recognize her if she surfaces again. A surveillance drone is in place for when she does."

The DD paced at the head of the table and looked straight at Bill. "Okay, let's say she is involved in orchestrating this. Do we know how she got the information?"

Bill sat up straight. "No sir."

"Then we need to concentrate on second-level investigations. Someone turned over that file." He poured more coffee into his cup and hesitated. "What are we doing to help the families?"

Bill stared at his folded hands on the table while he spoke. "Out of the nine names on the cover sheet, only the Jennings family is dead. We made arrangements to bring Jennings home. We have counselors in place, and people to assist with funeral arrangements and any other needed services. The Campbell family has additional security watching the house. The three other men who are in Syria have been warned, and their families are under extra detail at Fort Meade.

"Davis and Jessica have been set up with temporary residences nearby, and were told to alert their families to possible threats—even though the threat level is low, due to the fact their families are scattered out of state. That leaves your family members, sir, who have been moved to a Maryland location, and mine, who are currently en route. Live surveillance is monitoring each of their permanent addresses in case they are targeted."

The DD let out a heavy sigh. "Then at least we can stop the body count. The big question remains—why that file? They have all the government employees' information from that hack. The list they keep crossing off and leaving at the crime scenes is only from the file's cover sheet."

A silent pause fell around the table.

The Deputy Director leaned against the table and crossed his arms. "Do we have any new information that might explain why *that* file? It doesn't make sense to me. Why that one?"

Bill and Jessica shook their heads. "No idea, sir."

The Deputy Director's face was grim, his jaw muscles rippling. "Jessica, you are dismissed. Bill, I'd like to talk to you for a moment."

Jessica picked up her files without making eye contact with Bill. "Thank you, sir."

The Deputy Director closed the door behind Jessica and turned to Bill. "I understand there is a breach of trust between you and Jessica."

"You could say that, sir."

The DD put his hand in his pocket and slid Bill's phone across the table. Bill picked up the phone with a nod of acknowledgment that he was cleared of suspicion.

"I understand your lack of trust of Jessica, but I want to reassure you that she passed her polygraph. I called Agent Liam Garrison's supervisor earlier, and he assures me that they assigned him based solely on his boating experience. They also said Jessica was an excellent field agent and behaved professionally at all times. She made the decision to leave after she became involved with Garrison. She has ten years of outstanding service with the Bureau. They both do."

Silence filled the pause.

"Bill, she made a poor choice calling Agent Garrison today, but I'm convinced she was collecting intelligence on you. She wants to find the leak. Even so, she will be reprimanded for making a personal call on a secure line. You need to get past this and work together. We need to focus on all secondary investigations, and you two have to work as a team."

Bill ground his teeth while he listened to the Deputy Director. "Yes, sir."

The DD sighed. "Bill, we've known each other a long time. Don't do this."

Bill stared defiantly at the Deputy Director. "He still has my wife. And I haven't heard a thing all day, other than two men were spotted chasing after my boat on jet skis and were stopped by gunshots."

The DD glanced at his watch, 6:40 p.m. "He is due to report in from the TSL within the half hour. I'll include you in that information loop, and will instruct him to contact you personally as soon as we are finished."

The frown lines on Bill's forehead relaxed and his jaw slackened. "Thank you. That would be a big relief."

"I'm told the TSL is down around St. Michaels. The plan was to dock the boat at the pier since it's very remote by car. We can have a car drive you and Emma down there tonight, since it's a little less than three hours from here. You can work from your secure laptop, then report back here."

Bill's shoulders relaxed, and his stress level dropped at the news. He would see his family and get some needed sleep. And he would have time to calm down before he had to deal with Jessica again.

He shook the DD's hand. "Thank you, Gene."

***

Emma's knees were shaking when she took a seat at a long polished conference table in a windowless room. Four agents were there to listen to her story.

Emma peered nervously through her lashes at the three agents leaning against the wall. She squirmed in her seat under their stares.

The female agent sitting next to her introduced the other three agents before she began taking notes and asking questions. Each agent was gathering intelligence for different areas of the investigation.

"Emma, would you like some water before we get started?"

Emma nodded and licked her dry lips. "Yes, thank you."

"Let's start at the beginning of your day."

She began with her finals and meeting up with Blake. It was hard to believe that just a few short hours ago she was carefree and hanging out with her friends at the bar. Her eyes teared at the thought of him, and she gulped the bottle of water they provided.

She cleared her throat to strengthen her wobbling voice and continued telling her story about meeting her friends at the bar.

"Can you tell me the names of all the people you knew who were in the bar at that time?"

Emma began listing all her friends' names, and how they could be contacted.

"Anything or anyone else you can remember about the bar?"

Emma mentally revisited the afternoon at the bar. "Oh, and my neighbor Cal was at the bar. And again at the marina."

The agents drilled her story over and over. "Did anyone follow you from the bar?"

"I don't think so. Cal maybe followed us out. I remember him outside on the sidewalk talking on the phone when we left...and the same thing at the marina."

The agents exchanged a quick glance. No one had told her Cal was involved.

Holly, the female agent sitting next to Emma, rubbed her arm affectionately. "Emma, I know the rest of this is going to be hard, and if you need to take a break, just let us know.

Emma swallowed the lump in her throat and nodded.

"What can you tell us about the men at your house?"

Emma described them with as much detail as she could remember. "They said they wanted to use me to make a video." Her shoulders shook with an uncontrollable shudder.

Holly scribbled notes on her pad. "Do you think they were the same guys at the marina?"

"Maybe. I just didn't get a good look. But I think so."

Holly rubbed Emma's back. "You are doing great. Every detail you can give us gets us that much closer to bagging these creeps."

"The one who grabbed me at the house was hurt. I got him pretty good with the fire extinguisher on the head and dropped him with a final blow where it counts with a broom. I left him on the floor screaming, with wasp spray in his eyes."

One of the agents leaning against the wall grinned.

"Good for you. We know they were driving a cable van. Do you remember seeing one around your house before today?"

Emma thought back over the week, and remembered her roommate asking her something about the cable. *What was it? Something about whether we transferred the name on the cable bill?*

"I don't remember, but my roommate might have. She asked me something about the cable bill earlier this week."

Toward the end of the interview, they asked Emma if she had any questions.

Emma bit her lip and took a deep breath, steeling herself for their answer. "Where is Blake? What happened to him? Do his parents know?"

The agents glanced around the group, and Holly cleared her throat. "He was killed in the alley. His body is at the morgue. His parents were notified, and I'm sure they are making arrangements."

Emma's voice broke. "Do they know he was with me? That he died because of me?"

"I'm not sure."

Silence settled around the table.

Holly took Emma's hand. "Something terrible happened to you today. But it wasn't your fault. There was nothing you could have done to save Blake. You did the only thing you could have done. You were brave. If you had taken any other course of action, you both would be dead."

Emma closed her eyes to stifle the tears. "I feel so guilty for bringing him with me to the house."

The agent squeezed Emma's hand. "Don't. You didn't know what you were walking into. No one blames you."

Chapter 14
The Inquisition

Monday, May 9th, 5:30 p.m.

Larry climbed into the ambulance and tossed off a clipped farewell salute to Rondie through the back window.

He folded down the little shelf at the bottom of the beds and took a seat. "What do we have?"

The EMT put pressure bandages on their wounds and checked their vitals. He pointed to the shoulder wound. "Pulse and blood pressure don't indicate any arterial damage." Then pointed to the guy handcuffed in the other bed. "This guy's vitals are still all over the place from being tasered. The shot to the knee is more complicated. He'll need surgery."

Larry addressed the two men in a sympathetic tone. "You two have some kind of beef with that girl?"

Nothing.

"You know, the judge will go much easier on you if I can tell them you cooperated with me. Did someone put you up to this? You'll get a lot less time if you can show this wasn't your idea."

The guy with the shoulder wound shouted at the other. "Keep your mouth shut!"

Larry shrugged. "You two are on the security footage from The Crab House. We've been tracking you all morning."

The other guy was groaning in pain holding his bloody, busted knee. "I told you we shouldn't trust that bitch!"

Larry's eyebrows shot up at the idea a woman was behind the attack. "Why did she want you to hurt the girl?"

The first one reared his head up, fighting against the restraints and tearing open his shoulder wound further. "*Shut up!*"

"She wanted us to grab the girl. No one was supposed to get hurt."

Larry squatted next to the one talking. "Why did she want you to grab the girl?"

"Shut up, you fool!"

Larry raised his brows at the EMT and cocked his head at the shoulder wound. The EMT slipped a mouth guard for seizures into the mouth of the guy with the shoulder wound.

"What did she want with the girl?"

"She's on some list."

The shoulder wound spit out the guard. "You are going to get us killed. *Shut up!*"

Larry calmly continued. "How do you know Cal?"

"I don't know him."

"Why was he there?"

"Probably because of that bitch."

"Does the bitch have a name? What can you tell me about her?"

"She's got a list of people she says need to die because they are killing her people."

"Who are her people?"

"Syrians? ISIL? I don't know. How much longer 'til we get to the hospital?"

The one with the shoulder wound was almost convulsing with rage. "*You idiot!* You are as good as dead."

The EMT driving the ambulance looked into the rearview mirror at Larry. "Sir, I'm almost to the hospital. Do you want me to circle around for a bit?"

The knee wound pleaded, "I've told you everything, man. I need a doctor."

Larry made a few calls and was met by security when they pulled into the emergency entrance. He briefed the guards on protocol, then called Mo and Curly.

***

It was still drizzling at the marina's restaurant when Rondie jumped into the back of Mo and Curly's SUV. "What's the plan, boys?"

Mo glanced at her in the rearview mirror. "We're looking for their ride. Cable van was reported in the alley behind the house in Georgetown."

They rolled down the street slowly to where a cable van was parked. She hopped out and pulled at the magnetic sign on the side of the van. "Well, what do you know? This isn't really a cable van."

They jimmied the lock on the back and opened the door. Agent Monroe jumped in the back of the van and rifled through the contents. "My money says these are the guys from Georgetown." He picked up the dark hoodie. "Fits the description, and there is blood all over it. Call in a tow. Let's get the lab guys on this."

Rondie decided not to wait around for the chaos a crime scene created. She walked back to her boat and moved it back to her slip. She turned on her computer to see if she could track her phone.

After the phone call Emma made to Karen earlier, the GPS tracker disappeared. The app still couldn't locate her phone, so she surfed around the news and caught up on her email.

The young men she shot in the parking lot weighed on her mind. What if someone would have reached out to them when they were younger? Would they have taken a different path? She inhaled slowly and let out a deep sigh, looking out at the water. She had been on the wrong path in high school when someone gave her a second chance.

Rondie's mother died when she was fourteen, leaving her pretty much on her own. The strong sense of right and wrong her mother had instilled in her wavered while she watched her father resort to the bottle to cope.

A few caring teachers and her good grades floated her through to her senior year. But then she got mixed up with the wrong crowd. Juvenile delinquency, promiscuity, and alcohol put her on a fast track to trouble. A juvenile officer gave her an ultimatum of jail or the National Guard. She made tracks to the recruiter's office and planned to travel the world.

She rubbed at the scar that cut across her left hand. She had almost lost her hand when a tank hatch slammed shut behind her. Due to her carelessness, it also slammed shut on one of the few men who had befriended her, tearing through his left shoulder. It had been a hard lesson, but she never again forgot how much teamwork, precision, and hard work mattered.

Second chances. She remembered giving another young man a second chance, almost thirty years ago. It had gone very wrong. She should have killed him when she had the chance. If she had, a young mother wouldn't have been raped and murdered in front of her toddler. Her stomach turned at the memory. She had learned a valuable lesson then, too—not everyone deserves a second chance.

Rondie shook the memory away, and decided to call it a day and head home. She reached over to shut off the computer when an alert popped up, tracking her phone again.

***

The two agents pulled into the hospital parking lot and met Larry. They had been instructed to take the two patients to *The Barn* for questioning when they were able to move.

The Barn was located east of DC in Maryland. It was an idyllic location, surrounded by woods and horse farms. But inside the metal pole barn were rooms with metal rings and chains bolted into the concrete basement walls and floors. Special Forces were responsible for interrogation, and their methods often teetered on the edge of the Geneva Convention.

Curly turned toward to the backseat when Larry got back in the SUV. "Did you get any information from them on the ride over?"

"Not much. They are ISIL sympathizers, American, and probably wannabe copycats. They aren't the leaders. They referred to a *she* as the leader," said Larry.

Mo shook his head. "That makes no sense. ISIL isn't going to put a woman in charge."

Curly nodded and asked, "Did he say how many were involved?"

"Not really." Larry rubbed the back of his neck. "I'm guessing less than six."

Mo sat forward with his hands clasped between his knees. "Are they the same two from the jet skis?"

"I think so. I told them The Crab House had video of them, and one started to comment before the other shut him up. We need to get them separated and questioned before lawyers show up," said Larry.

Chapter 15
Leak stopped

Monday, May 9th, 6:15 p.m.

Liam couldn't leave the boat. The storm wasn't letting up. The bilge pump alarm was still buzzing, and the water level didn't appear to be receding. He looked at the clock. 6:15 p.m. Where was Karen? She had been gone a long time.

Liam cupped his hands and shouted against the wind, "Hey kid!"

The dock boy's umbrella flipped backward in the wind as he approached the boat.

"What happened to the woman who got off this boat?"

The kid shrugged his shoulders and pursed his lips to the side. "I dunno."

"Is the dockmaster here? I need this boat pulled."

"If he is, he would be down there." He pointed down the little canal with the rip-rap rocks on one side and boat slips on the other.

Liam was torn between the sinking boat and his missing charge. Screwing up either one would mean the Assistant Director transferring him to hell.

"Can you call him? Tell him it's an emergency. This boat is sinking."

***

Jerry, the dockmaster, was in the marina restaurant with a couple of guys who worked for the marina when his phone rang. They were watching the storm on the screen over the bar.

"Yeah, this is Jerry."

"This is Justin at the gas dock. I got this guy down here says his boat is sinking and he needs it pulled. We've been using the pump-out to pump out the water."

Jerry rolled his eyes. "Put him on the phone."

Justin trudged back through the rain to Liam and handed him his phone through the side window of the boat.

Liam reached for the phone and shouted over the storm. "Hello?"

"Kid says you got a problem?"

"Dripless shaft seal let go."

Jerry chuckled. "That is a problem. What size is the shaft?"

Liam rubbed his chin. "I think it's an inch and a half."

Jerry slid off his barstool and pulled up the hood on his raincoat. "Let me grab a pump. I've got a jury-rigged clamp and hoses that I think'll work."

Liam saw the water sloshing close to the engines. "Can't we pull it?"

"Not in this storm. We'll have to drain the water, or it'll be too heavy and unstable. We'll move it to the service dock when the storm passes."

Liam sighed heavily. "It's hooked up to the pump-out now, but the boat is taking on water faster than it's pumping it out."

Jerry grunted. "That pump isn't going to do what you need. I'll be down. This will work."

Five minutes later, Jerry climbed aboard with a gas-powered pump, and the water started pouring out like an open fire hydrant. The water level was visibly receding inch by inch.

Jerry swiped at a white blob that was about to get sucked into the pump and yelled over the bilge alarm blaring in the background. "Is this what it looks like?"

Liam shook his head and started scooping up the white blobs. "Don't ask."

Jerry grabbed the clamp he had previously fabricated. He hadn't had an opportunity to try it out, and was anxious to see if it would work. He pulled at the plastic sacks attached to the duct tape and pads. "What the hell?" He threw them at Liam like they were on fire before attaching his clamp. The incoming water immediately slowed to a small trickle.

Jerry stood and wiped his hands on his pants with satisfaction. "Okay, this ought to hold it. Let's finish pumping and then move it over to the service dock."

Liam nodded and ran his fingers through his hair with relief. "Thanks, man. You're a lifesaver."

Jerry climbed up the engine room ladder. "Not a problem. Storm should blow over in another thirty minutes or so. You can find me in the bar."

Liam shook Jerry's hand. "Thanks again. Hey, have you seen the woman who got off this boat?"

Jerry's bushy brows pinched with concern. "Yeah. She took a nasty tumble. When she came into the restaurant, her knees were scraped up and bleeding. One of the gals pointed it out, and when she looked down, she just passed out. The girls took her back to the shower rooms. I didn't see her come out."

Liam's eyes shot wide open with panic, and he followed Jerry out onto the deck.

Jerry yelled at the dockboy. "Justin!"

The kid poked his head out into the rain. "Yeah?"

"Come here and keep an eye on this until he gets back."

Liam shook out a folded slicker from the side pocket of his rucksack, put it on, and hefted the bag over his shoulder. Then he followed Jerry to the marina restaurant to find Karen. The restaurant had a few people sitting around the bar and a huddle of waitresses at the far wall of windows watching the storm.

Jerry called to the bartender. "Where's that woman who came in here with bloody knees?"

The bartender pointed down the hall toward the marina shower rooms. Liam headed down the hall and knocked on the door labeled Women. "Karen? You in there?"

The young long-legged waitress who was helping Karen opened the door. A slow grin lit up her face when she saw Liam. She gave him a flirty smile and asked, "Is this your mom?"

Liam heard Karen gasp behind the girl. "Mother!"

Liam tried to hide his smile. "No, that's not my mom. Just a friend."

The girl opened the door wide. "You can come on in."

Karen was sitting on a shower bench. She had cleaned her legs and was holding clean white gauze against them. "Is the boat still afloat?"

Liam bent down in front of Karen and rested his bag on the floor behind him. "Yeah, it'll be okay. Can I take a look?"

Karen winced and pulled back the gauze.

Liam chewed the side of his mouth as he examined her knees. "You've got some splinters embedded in both knees, and they could both use stitches."

Karen leaned her head against the wall. "The Anne Arundel Medical Clinic is about fifteen minutes from here."

Liam stared at her and silently tried to communicate they couldn't give away their location. He looked at the young girl's nametag. "Carly?"

Carly smiled and stepped closer. "Yeah?"

"Could you give us a few minutes alone and just stand outside, so I don't startle anyone wanting to use the restroom?"

Carly smiled, seeming pleased to be helpful, and stepped outside.

Karen held up her palms. "Well?"

"We can't go to a public hospital. Your information and location will be tracked immediately. We are due to check in at a TSL within the next half hour. I'll call and make other arrangements. They'll send a car and make secure arrangements for you to get stitched up."

"What about the boat?"

"Is there anything valuable on there we need to take with us if we leave it here?"

Karen thought about what was on the boat. "I don't know. I need to talk to Bill."

Liam stood and rubbed his face. "This is such a cluster f—." He caught himself midsentence. Sucking in a deep breath, he pulled out his phone and checked the time, 6:45 p.m. He punched in the numbers. "I'll call."

After a pause, he said, "This is Osprey 1 calling for assistance."

He heard some clicks on the other end of the line, then heard, "Go ahead, Liam. The line is secure. What's going on?"

"I'm on the Eastern Shore at the Kentmoor Marina. The boat took on water, and we had to dock it. We will need transportation to the TSL. The Assistant Director's wife fell and needs minor medical attention. Possible stitches."

"Standby, Liam. I have a message that the Assistant Director wants to talk directly to you. You are to call him at this number." She gave Liam the number, and he committed it to memory.

Liam muttered "*shit*" under his breath while he punched in the AD's number.

Chapter 16
Temporary Truce

Monday, May 9th, 6:45 p.m.

Bill walked back to his office and was briefing his secretary on the arrangements for the next few days when his cell phone rang.

"Hello?"

"Sir, this is Agent Garrison. I was told to call you direct with an update."

Bill walked into his office and sat down. "Call back on my landline, please." He gave him the number, ended the call, and waited.

Thirty seconds later, Bill answered his landline.

"Are you at the TSL?"

"Uh…no, sir, we're over on the Eastern Shore at the Kentmoor Marina. We've had a problem."

"Is my wife okay?"

"Uh…yes, sir, but she fell and probably needs stitches in both knees."

"Is she there? May I talk to her?"

"Yes, sir. I'll put her on." Liam handed the phone to Karen. "It's your husband."

Karen grabbed the phone. "Bill! Where are you? What the hell is going on? Have you talked to Emma?"

"I have Emma. She's being interviewed right now or I'd put her on the phone. Are you okay, Karen?"

Karen squeezed her eyes shut to stifle her tears but was unable to hold back the sob of relief from Emma being found. She drew in a deep breath and exhaled slowly. Her voice still quivered when she asked, "Is Emma okay? Where did you find her?"

"She's fine Karen. Don't worry. I'll fill you in on all the details when I see you. Are you okay?"

"I…I think so. I fell getting off that damn boat in this storm. It took on water, and we're just lucky it didn't sink!"

Bill rubbed his forehead with frustration at the mention of the boat. "Where's the boat now?"

Karen looked at Liam. "I think it's at the dock getting pumped out."

Liam nodded his head and mouthed, "I'll need to talk to him."

"Liam says he needs to speak with you." She handed the phone back to him. "Here."

"Yes, sir. About the boat. The dripless shaft seal let go. It's getting pumped out. Dock master clamped it, but the boat is going to need pulled when the storm clears. We need to get a car and get to the TSL."

Bill closed his eyes and ran his hand over his face. "Okay. I was going to drive there tonight with my daughter. Um…let me make arrangements with the dockmaster. I'll take care of the boat from here. Has your location been blown?"

"No sir. I don't think so." Liam turned to Karen. "Did you tell anyone your name?"

Karen shook her head. "No, I passed out before anyone asked."

"Other than the name on your boat, no one knows who we are."

"Okay, we'll send a car and make arrangements at the Anne Arundel Medical Center on Kent Island. I'll meet you at the TSL tonight."

"Okay, thank you, sir. Do you want to talk to your wife again?"

"Yes, thank you, Agent Garrison."

Karen held the phone to her ear. "What is going on?'

"I'm sending a car to take you to the medical center on Kent Island. I'll meet you later at the Temporary Secure Location. You'll like it, it's nice, and I'm bringing Emma with me. She's been through so much today. Have you been listening to the news?"

Karen huffed indignantly at the idea that she'd had time to sit around and watch TV. "No, I've been busy with your damn boat! What happened to Emma?"

"Karen, I promise, I'll tell you everything when I see you. She's fine. Don't worry."

Bill hung up the phone and leaned back in his chair, closing his eyes and giving a silent prayer of gratitude. He jotted down a list of calls he needed to make. The first call was to Jessica.

"Jessica, can you come to my office?"

"Be right there, sir."

Jessica knocked timidly on Bill's open door. "What's up?"

He quickly related the situation with Karen, and put Jessica in charge of setting up the car and making the medical arrangements. When she left, he called the dockmaster at the marina to check up on his boat and make the necessary arrangements to have it pulled and dry-docked.

Jessica was back at his door twenty minutes later. She had worked fast to carry out his orders and make amends.

"Sir?"

Bill looked up at the innocent expression on Jessica's face. He waved her into his office.

Jessica delved right into her arrangements. "I have a car being delivered to Agent Garrison at the marina. It should be there now. If not, it will be within minutes. The medical center was alerted, and Mrs. Carr will see a doctor immediately, without a footprint. Your TSL would take you over the Bay Bridge by car. That creates vulnerabilities that leave few options if something were to happen on the bridge. But we got lucky. The FBI scheduled night training on top of the Hoover Building tonight. They will pick you and Emma up on the helipad at 8:30 tonight and take you to meet Agent Garrison at the Easton Airport, where he will transport you to the TSL."

Bill knew Jessica had worked hard to get all that accomplished in such a short amount of time. He looked at her two-day-old outfit and red eyes.

"Thank you, Jessica." He ran his hand over his face. "We're under a lot of pressure and running on no sleep. A lot of unkind things have been said between us. I apologize. I want you to go to your TSL and get some sleep. We'll keep in touch through a secure line."

"Thank you, Bill. My TSL is minutes from here, so I can be here in an instant if you need me."

Bill nodded. "Good to know."

Jessica hesitated. "You know Bill…I've been thinking."

Bill raised his brows. "Yeah?"

"There hasn't been any chatter or movement within the actual operation in Syria. I got word the agents were pulled a little while ago, and nothing has changed. No one has noticed any changes."

"That's good."

"True, but don't you think if someone knew all about the op, they would do *something*? Why haven't we seen *any* movement over there?"

Bill sat back down and ran his hands over his face. "I hadn't thought of that. There hasn't been *any* noticeable difference in the op?"

Jessica shook her head.

Bill raised his left brow. "What are you suggesting?"

Jessica sat back in the chair and crossed her leg. "I'm wondering if this is just a lucky guess on someone's part. They put together the names of agents who have worked together before, or something, and the government's OPM leak gave them the agent's addresses."

Bill nodded along as Jessica kicked around different theories. He tilted his head. "It's been *total* silence?"

Jessica nodded. "Yep. Nothing and no one has changed positions, other than our guys."

Bill's brows furrowed as he made some notes. "Hmm. Well, I'm due to be briefed on Emma's ordeal right now. You are welcome to sit in with me."

Jessica smiled. "Thanks."

Bill and Jessica stood and walked amicably to the briefing—the first glimmer of a truce shown all day.

Chapter 17
The Accident

Monday, May 9th, 7:00 p.m.

Karen stood next to Liam at the bar, half listening to his conversation with the dockmaster, discussing the details about pulling the boat. Breaking news was flashing on the television behind him, and the President came on.

Karen strained to hear the broadcast. "Hey, could you turn that up?"

The bartender turned up the TV, and leaned against the bar to hear the special news report.

The President stood behind a podium in the Roosevelt room. "Good afternoon. I want to reassure the American citizens that the two earlier attacks in DC have been contained, and we have three suspects in custody. I want to be clear. We have no specific and credible intelligence plots against the homeland. However, as a precaution, we are stepping up security at Metro, and adjusting tactical units where necessary. We are continuing to monitor and secure our posture using combined military and Homeland Security efforts. You will be informed if we have a known credible threat, but for now, if you see something suspicious, say something. The most important thing you can do right now is go about your normal routines."

She stopped listening and turned toward the door when two men walked in wearing dark suits.

Liam smiled and extended his hand. "Hey, our ride is here."

The taller of the two agents shook Liam's hand and gave him a set of keys. "Hey, Liam, good to see you. You've got a black SUV waiting outside. I'm catching a ride back with Gary."

"Okay, thanks." Liam turned to Karen. "You ready?"

"I'm going to grab a few things off the boat; I'll be right back."

Liam groaned impatiently. "Just leave it. We need to get out of here. The doc is waiting for us, and we need to get to the TSL before dark."

"No. I'm getting my BOB bag. It's got stuff I need."

"Trust me, you won't need it. The TSL will have everything you need."

Karen turned toward the pier. "I'll just be a minute. Wait for me in the car."

Liam hesitated, but saw the determination in Karen's eyes and just threw up his hands in defeat. "Make it quick."

The rain had let up to a sprinkle when she boarded the boat. She went into her little closet and stripped out of the wet clothes and put on dry underwear, T-shirt and sweats. She stepped down into the galley and grabbed her BOB bag from the table. When she passed through the cabin, she saw Rondie's phone and battery on the counter. She peeked out the window to see where Liam was and then put in the phone's battery.

She called Emma's phone. Voicemail. The only other phone number she had memorized was her neighbor. Anxious for information, she decided to give her neighbor Peggy a quick call to see if she had been listening to the news Bill referred to earlier. "Hey, Peggy it's me, Karen." She heard loud talking and lots of commotion in the background. "What's going on?"

Peggy screamed into the phone. "What has your daughter gotten my son involved in?"

"What are you talking about?"

"Emma's name has been all over the news. Don't play dumb. She accused Cal of being part of some gang. The police are here searching my house, and Cal is in *jail*!"

"Peggy, what are you talking about?" Karen looked up and saw Liam coming down the dock. "I have to go. We'll get this straightened out when I get home." She ended the call and shoved the phone in her BOB bag, hitching it over her shoulder and walking out on deck just as Liam reached the boat.

"What's taking you so long?"

Karen opened her rain slicker and pointed at her dry clothes. "I had to get out of my wet clothes."

Liam held his hand up to help her off the boat.

Karen accepted his gesture. "Thank you."

They walked out to the car in silence. Once in the car, Liam programmed the navigation system with their destination and said, "These back roads will be tricky at night. There won't be any street signs or lights."

Karen's brow was knit with worry. "I hope this doctor visit is quick." She peered out the window while Liam put the SUV in gear and pulled out of the marina. They were in a heavily wooded area, and were approaching a swollen creek covered by a quaint old bridge. There was no traffic. She was staring out into the trees when Liam's arm flew out and braced her across her chest.

Liam stomped on the brakes and yelled, "*Hang on!*"

She turned forward and screamed when she saw an enormous buck smash into the windshield and felt the SUV spin out of control on the wet pavement. Liam tried to correct his sharp swerve, but the car hydroplaned and headed down the embankment where they rolled over and over until the car stopped.

Karen wasn't sure how long she had been unconscious when she opened her eyes. It was dark. There was glass all around her, and the sides of the SUV were caved in around them. She turned her head to the side and looked out her window, but all she could see was dirt and grass. Liam's side was the same. Were they in a ditch?

She could hear rushing water. The bloody legs and hooves of the buck were poking through the windshield. Her airbag was between her and the deer.

Liam was still unconscious and had a gash in his hair that was bleeding down the side of his face. His shoulder was sticking out from the seatbelt at an odd angle, and was probably dislocated.

She wiggled her feet and ankles. No broken bones.

Her neck was sore, but she could move her head back and forth.

She wiggled her fingers and flexed her arms. Nothing appeared broken. She sucked in her stomach to create space and slowly squeezed her arm down between the airbag and seat to unhook her seatbelt. Every movement created excruciating pain, but she needed to pop the airbag so she could move around.

The sound of water was getting louder. Adrenaline kicked in at the thought of drowning. She knew there was a pocketknife in the side of her BOB bag if she could just get to it. It was sitting next to her knee, just inches from her hand. She leaned against the door with all her weight and stretched her hand until she felt the bag. She rocked back and forth, inching her way down. Her legs had more movement. She knocked the bag with the side of her knee, moving it closer to her hand.

"Yes!" She wrapped her fingers around the handle and pulled. She wasn't sure if it was her imagination or if the water was getting louder. She slid her fingers along the side of her bag and found something hard and metal. She wrapped her fingers around it and pulled hard, freeing it from the pocket.

She slowly leaned back to the middle console, pulling up the object in her hand. When she was finally able to get her hand to her lap, she realized it was a corkscrew. She struggled to pull the cover off the curly metal and pushed the pointed end into the airbag.

When nothing much happened, she poked more holes into the bag. Small leaks began to deflate the bag, allowing her more and more movement. The clock flashed on the dash while the airbag shrank, 9:00.

"Liam!" She pulled her arm free of the bag and reached over to shake him, careful of his shoulder. "Liam!"

He groaned, but his eyes were still closed.

"Liam! We're in a ditch, and there's water coming in. We need to get out."

Her ribs were throbbing in pain with every breath. She rolled down the airbag, pushing the air out. Free of the seatbelt and airbag, she reached for the BOB bag and found the knife. She leaned across to Liam and slashed his airbag, giving him more room to move. Still nothing.

Next, she laid on the horn for a full minute, until Liam lifted his good arm and grabbed her wrist. "Stop!"

"Liam we are wedged in a ditch, and we've gotta get out of here. You're hurt. You've got blood running down your head and your shoulder is…messed up."

Liam tried to lean forward but fell back against the headrest wincing in pain.

She laid on the horn again, hoping someone would hear and bring help.

Liam put a death grip on her wrist and glared at her. "Stop!"

Karen peeled his fingers from her wrist and sat back to take stock of their surroundings. She caught a movement out of the corner of her eye. She turned toward the movement and pushed back against the seat, shielding her face when the deer woke up and thrashed against the windshield, kicking glass all over them. The deer caught some traction against the dash and struggled to its feet before leaping out of the ditch.

Karen put her hand over her pounding heart. "Whoa!" She noticed the sunroof and leaned over Liam's lap to find the button to open it.

A small grin played around Liam's lips. "Hey, what makes you think I'm that kinda guy?"

Karen rolled her eyes. "Shut up! I thought you were too hurt to move."

He grinned wider. "Some movements are just involuntary."

"Aagh! Men!" The sunroof opened, dumping rocks and debris on top of them. Karen sat back in her seat and held her aching ribs, sweat rolling down her face. She was resting, gathering the strength to crawl out through the sunroof.

"Can you move?"

Liam stretched his good arm forward and grabbed the handle. He pulled his body forward and tried to straighten using his feet, but stopped quickly. "I think my ankle is sprained."

"I'm calling an ambulance."

He shook his head from side to side. "No."

Karen threw up her hands. "Don't be ridiculous! We need help!"

"Get my phone. It's in my pants pocket."

Karen gave Liam a suspicious look, pursed her lips and asked sarcastically, "Which pocket is it in?"

Liam wrapped his good arm around his ribs and coughed. "Don't make me laugh. It hurts. It's in my right front pocket."

Karen was fishing around in his pocket, when she froze at the sound of a gunshot.

Liam's eyes cut to the side without moving his head. He closed his eyes and moaned, "Oh shit!"

Chapter 18
Questions

Monday, May 9th, 9:00 p.m.

Bill couldn't concentrate on reading the reports in front of him. He was still reeling from the briefing on the news that the neighbor boy was involved with the attack on Emma. How many times had Karen and Peggy sat out by the pool or socialized at different events? They had been good friends and neighbors for the past ten years. Cal was thirteen when they moved in. He seemed polite, smart, and well behaved. How could something like this happen in his own backyard? Did Cal have something against his family? Did he have a grudge against Emma?

He asked to be briefed the moment the search turned up anything at the neighbor's house. So far, the parents and younger sibling were reported as being clueless. If that was the case, he felt sorry for the family, because their life would never be the same. Every move and email would be scrutinized, and they would live their life under a cloud of suspicion.

What could have been Cal's motivation? Money? Retribution? He ran his hand over his face and sighed. Cal always seemed like a smart kid. Good-looking. Never saw him with a girl. Well dressed. Quiet.

He could just see the headlines. *Assistant Director in the FBI was clueless about the terrorist living next door to him.* He shook his head. How many other people are living next door to terrorists?

He glanced at the clock on the wall for the thousandth time, 9:00 p.m. Karen was supposed to have called from the TSL more than an hour ago. The last intelligence anyone had regarding her and Liam was at the marina. They hadn't visited the doctor. Where were they?

He glanced out his door at Jessica's empty office. Was it a coincidence she left at the same time his wife went missing? Was she involved in this mess? He rubbed his hand over his face. Was his lack of sleep causing paranoia? Jessica told him she was going to get some sleep.

Bill leaned back in his chair and closed his eyes. His mind wouldn't slow down. He ran through the timeline of events, beginning two days ago, when Jessica last logged into the file.

Yesterday – an ISIL threat claiming retaliation. Common enough to throw on the pile.

Last night – a specific threat naming nine people involved in a highly classified Syrian Operation. They had worked through the night corroborating intelligence and putting the different law enforcement agencies on alert.

5:30 this morning – Campbell's home has attempted break-in, and a note is found confirming the family is targeted.

About the same time – Jennings family is murdered in Bethesda.

11:30 or so, Agent Garrison joined Karen on the boat. Two guys on jet skis are reported by the waitress at The Crab House chasing the boat.

2:00 Blake is stabbed and two guys escape in a van. More than likely the same guys at the marina.

4:00 Emma and Rondie are attacked by the same two guys at the marina. Cal is picked up.

Around 7:00, he talked to Karen and Agent Garrison on the Eastern Shore.

He looked at the clock—9:05. *Where were they?*

He sighed and waded through the pile of reports on his desk, sorting information relating to the attacks by priority into different piles to brief the Director.

- Three of the men known to have participated in the attacks are in custody. Preliminary reports show two of the three are Americans who became radicalized for the ISIL cause. ISIL sympathizers trying to copycat? An isolated cell?

- The #702 Op is still in place, and no known intelligence indicates the location or operation should change.

- Those named on the cover sheet had been moved and provided with new covers.

Bill ran his hand over his face, as was his nervous habit, and thought about Karen again. *The doctor at the Anna Arundel Medical Center said they never showed. There has been no trace of the car they are driving, and no one has been to the TSL. Where are they?*

Where is Jessica? He had tasked Agent Marcs with locating Jessica an hour ago. She hasn't answered her phone or texts in hours. What if she and Garrison are working together? What if they took Karen?

Bill's thoughts were interrupted by a knock on his door, and Emma walked into his office. "Hi, Dad."

"Hi, honey. Is the interrogation finished?"

"I think so. I can't think of anything else to tell them. When are we going to see Mom?"

Bill sighed and chose his words carefully. "We might have a change in plans. I'm still waiting to hear from your Mom."

"So I guess we aren't going in the helicopter?"

Bill frowned and shook his head. "No, they left at 8:30. They have arranged an apartment in DC for us. Do you want to go there and wait? I'm sure it has everything you need. You'll be much more comfortable there, and I'll call you when I hear what the plan is."

"By myself?"

"An agent will drive you there and escort you into the apartment, and double check it before he or she leaves. And another agent will be posted outside. You'll be fine."

Emma reluctantly shrugged. "Well, okay then." She walked to the door and stopped. "Dad, can I call Blake's parents or my friends? I need to talk to them. I'm sure everyone is going nuts after listening to the news."

Bill ran his hand down his face, unsure what to tell her. "You can use my phone to call Blake's parents, but I wish you'd hold off on your friends until we can get a better handle on things."

Emma swallowed. "Okay…Dad?" She cleared her throat and wiped at the tear rolling down her cheek. "What should I say to them?"

"Tell them how sorry you are, and let them know how much you cared for Blake. That he was a hero. He died protecting you."

Emma bit her lip and nodded, making no attempt to stop the tears streaking down her cheeks. Her voice was squeaky, and she looked like she was five years old. "I'm afraid they are going to hate me."

Bill walked around the desk and held her. "They've lost their son. They are entitled to whatever feelings they have. If the situation were reversed, and it had been you who died…" Bill swallowed the lump in his throat. "I would probably hate those involved too. It's part of the grieving process."

Silence fell between them. "The important thing is that you reach out to them and help them honor their son's memory."

Chapter 19
Lana

Monday, May 9th, 6:50 p.m.

The dinner crowd was thinning out at the sandwich shop across from the Bureau. A dozen or so people were sitting with earbuds plugged into their computers and eyes glued to the screens. People often ordered coffee and sat by the window for hours, using their laptops throughout the day.

A drop-dead gorgeous blonde walked through the door, attracting the attention of every male in the restaurant. Her tight jeans hugged her full bottom, and a low-cut T-shirt showed off her ample breasts. Her high heels clicked across the floor, where she joined the dark-haired young man sitting in the window with his laptop.

Ahmed cut his eyes to the side when she sat down, and spat, "Why you still wear your filthy American costume? Take out those ugly contacts."

Lana checked the area around them and gave him a plastered-on beauty pageant smile. "My burqa made me invisible in Syria, but here it is a neon sign, especially after San Bernardino. You think I should be in a hoodie and sneakers and carry a knife and backpack? No one looks at me when I'm like this."

"Everyone look at you!"

"They see a pretty American girl. Not an ISIL terrorist. You forget; we are not in Syria. Women dress as they want and have rights here."

Ahmed narrowed his eyes with hatred. "You send your stupid boyfriend to marina for getaway car?"

"Yes. I asked him to pick up my *friends*."

"Why he think he pick them up?"

Lana smiled smugly. "I tell him my friends have car trouble and need ride."

Ahmed rolled his eyes and sneered, "Stupid American."

Lana sat back in the chair, crossed her legs and swung her foot back and forth, with the heel of her sandal dangling from her red-manicured toes. "He cares for me."

She stared out the window at the FBI building, ruminating over their orders. Before they left Syria, she had convinced the ISIL leader that if her cover was a bossy American woman in charge, no one would look twice at her.

She had fought alongside them for the last three years, ever since she was fifteen. Killing and violence had been her whole life since she left Iraq and fled to Syria, hoping for a better life.

The others must not find out she left her targets alive on purpose. She had lost herself since she came to America—or had she found herself?

A father with his little girl walked past the window, triggering an almost-forgotten memory of her father. Her last memory of him. She had been nine years old, and they lived in Fallujah. The date stuck in her mind—April 28, 2003. Her father had kissed her and her mother goodbye and gone out after the American-enforced curfew. He told her he was going to join with other Fallujah citizens to demand the Americans vacate the secondary school building.

She waited anxiously with her mother all night, but her father never returned. She overheard her relatives the next day arguing about who started the fight with the American soldiers. Her uncle had been with her father, and he was telling the family that the protesters started throwing rocks and yelling at the American soldiers who were on top of the school roof. The soldiers threw smoke gas canisters down at the protesters to get them to leave. Next, he heard gunshots; then there was chaos and screaming. They were caught in a crossfire of bullets between the protesters and the soldiers when her father fell to the street, dead. Her uncle wasn't sure which side had killed her father.

At first, friends and what few relatives they had helped her and her mother, and life seemed to be returning to normal, despite sporadic bombings and growing anti-American sentiments. As months dragged on, she was forbidden to go to school because of "lightning raids" by American troops searching for insurgent activity in the schools.

Almost a year after her father's death, four American Blackwater contractors were killed, torched, and hung from a bridge. She rejoiced at the news and felt a sense of justice for her father's death. But her happiness was fleeting because, a few days later, fighting broke out all over Fallujah. Nothing made sense to a little girl when she heard phrases like Iraqi insurgency, guerrilla factions, Sunni rebellion, and coalition forces.

She remembered the night her relatives stayed up all night in the kitchen talking while airstrikes and gunfire boomed in the background—April 4, 2004. Two thousand American troops surrounded Fallujah. The next morning, her mother loaded her meager belongings on her back and set out with their relatives to flee Fallujah, but they found American troops had blockaded the roads with Humvees and concertina wire. The Americans were searching for those responsible for the Blackwater contractors' deaths. They waited until dark and had set out again to flee Fallujah when air bombardments rained down on the city, lighting the skies and killing her mother.

She was draped over her mother, sobbing, when someone pulled her up by her arm and dragged her through the streets and out into the desert. They walked all night. By morning, she was emotionally numb. She had lost her mother. She had no home. No family. And no clue how to survive.

Ahmed snapped his fingers in front of Lana's face. "You hear me?"

Lana pierced him with a death stare.

"The newscaster just reported that they have found a security video of a person of interest involved in an attempted break-in at an Alexandria home. It was believed to be a woman carrying a backpack, wearing a black hoodie and jogging pants. They were asking anyone with any information to call the number on the tip line."

He grabbed her arm with urgency. "Why you not kill them?"

Lana wrenched her arm away from him and sneered. "You forget to tell me they have dog. Before I could get in the house the woman called the police."

"You should have killed her anyway!"

"I couldn't see her. She was shouting from inside. You gave me bad information."

"You shouldn't have come. You shame Islam."

Lana turned her back on him and noticed the three young women sitting at the table next to them. They were talking about meeting later that night for drinks, and were kicking around names of area bars.

Lana looked at the one with the long brown hair and green eyes. She reminded her of Katie, the American she met in Syria who helped her with her English and explained different American ways and customs.

Katie had come over to join ISIL, expecting to fight for a humanitarian cause. She had been in their camp for a week before her first beating. She learned quickly not to speak or look a man in the eyes. They took her passport and used her to gain information about America.

When they were together at night, she would secretly help Lana with her English and tell her many stories of her home. Lana had left school at ten, but she was smart. She picked up the language, and remembered everything the young American girl had told her about how to dress, act, speak and interact with Americans.

In return, Lana told Katie how she came to be in the ISIL camp in Syria. She told her how her parents died in Iraq, and how she came to be lost, hungry, and begging in the streets. She was passed around for years among orphanages, and perverted men, then back to the streets. Eventually she was offered food and shelter by a group of thugs. Tired of fighting for survival on the streets, she accepted their protection, indebting herself to the radical, criminal group calling themselves ISIL.

Up until then, she had relied on her beauty to keep her alive. But after she joined ISIL, she discovered she had skills. She was one of their best sharpshooters, and a master of disguise. Her street smarts enabled her to combine her talents and manipulate the leaders until she secured a relatively secure position.

Lana admired the girl's purse and jeans at the next table. She thought how easy things were for American women. They had everything she wanted.

Her thoughts were interrupted when Ahmed elbowed her to look at a picture on his screen of the agent they were tracking. His eyes were wild when he nodded at Lana to look out the window. The picture on the screen matched the woman across the street. He jumped up, shoving his laptop in the carrying case.

She couldn't believe their good fortune! There was FBI Special Assistant Jessica Murphy, emerging from the Bureau's garage under an umbrella. They hurried out the door and were formulating a plan when Jessica walked right toward them.

Ahmed stepped into the alcove of the nearby store where they rented storage space.

Lana called out in her best American accent. "Hey, Jessica." For a split second, Lana wished she was really calling out to her beautiful American friend.

Jessica looked up from her phone, and Ahmed grabbed her from behind, covering her face with a cloth saturated with chloroform that he'd been carrying around in a plastic baggie. Lana rushed toward them, pretending to help a sick friend, and the two of them dragged her down the side stairs of their acquaintance's shop to the storage room.

"Put on your burqa before she wakes up. She can't see you."

Lana rolled her eyes. "She already did."

Ahmed raised his hand threateningly to her.

Lana sighed and slipped the suicide belt on under her burqa, ready to end things if they spun out of her control. She had kept the suicide belt in her backpack since she left Syria, vowing to die rather than being captured. She knew it was better to die on her own terms. Gruesome images of young girls being raped and tortured, fueled by her own experiences, haunted her.

She shook away her fears and concentrated on Cal. Those memories made her happy. She remembered when she first met him on an online dating site. She wanted to practice her English. They had chatted back and forth for almost two years, sharing personal thoughts and dreams.

He told her all about his family and school. When he told her he lived next door to an Assistant Director of the FBI, she began to pump him for information. He had never had a long-term girlfriend. He was painfully shy, and his good looks had always attracted unwanted attention, forcing him to become even more withdrawn. The online dating site was perfect for him, and he told her everything she ever wanted to know.

She dared to wonder what her life would have been like with Cal. It was unfathomable to imagine living the perfect American life as a wife with children and a house. A pang of remorse wafted over her as she pondered the plans she must help bring to completion. They couldn't be stopped now. She smoothed her furrowed brows and exhaled slowly.

Chapter 20
Kidnapped

Monday, May 9th, 7:00 p.m.

Jessica left the briefing with a sigh of relief, knowing the two men after Emma were in custody, and she and Bill were back on better terms. She was anxious to hear what the two men would reveal about the operation once they were at The Barn. She had little sympathy for them after seeing what they'd done to Emma's boyfriend, Blake.

She glanced out the window and saw the rain had slowed. Stretching her arms over her head, and longing for some exercise, she decided to walk the few short blocks to the apartment that had been arranged for her TSL, and get some needed sleep. She slipped on her tactical rain jacket and stepped into the elevator.

Jessica pushed up her umbrella with one hand and thumbed through her phone with the other when she left the building via the parking garage. She returned text messages to a couple of friends and then scrolled through her Instagram. Work tensions eased with every step closer to crawling into bed.

She walked past the sandwich shop and turned the corner when she heard someone call her name. She looked up to see a familiar face outside a tiny Indian storefront with bright clothing and accessories in the window. Before she could process who it was, someone grabbed her from behind, forcing a cloth over her nose and mouth. Her eyelids and muscles grew heavy while she was dragged down a set of stairs before passing out.

Some time later, Jessica heard a woman's voice talking in what sounded like Farsi. Her mind was foggy, so she forced herself to orient to her surroundings. She remembered being grabbed and pushed into a store. She slowly opened her eyes and realized she was blindfolded. She pulled against her restraints. Her wrists were taped to her ankles behind her back. A cloth was stuffed in her mouth and held fast with duct tape, and her nose stung from a bitter chemical.

She had trained for this moment. *Stay calm. Get to know your environment.* She was in a wet cardboard box that smelled like cat urine. Her clothes were wet. Two other people were in the room. A woman and a man. The man had a heavy accent. Loud construction noises were just outside. She could hear footsteps above and people talking. Indian music was playing in the background upstairs.

Her left arm was asleep, so she must have been lying on it for quite some time. She extended her fingers to her ankle holster. No gun. She ran her finger along the inside of the holster and felt the soft calfskin pocket for her small tactical knife. The knife slid easily from the holster, and she felt for the stud, careful not to deploy the powdered steel blade until it was in position, or she'd risk losing a finger.

She held it as far away from her body as possible and tapped the stud, releasing the blade. It sliced through the tape holding her hands and ankles together like butter. The immediate relief to her shoulders gave her more room to maneuver the knife. She waited for the cover of the pounding jackhammer outside to free her hands, then remove the gag, and push up the blindfold.

She carefully widened a tear in the wet cardboard so she could see her captors. A woman in a burqa was sitting on a folding chair under a barred basement window, using a cell phone. A scruffy-bearded dark-haired man in flip-flops and long shorts sat on the floor next to her typing on a laptop. The room was small and dank, boxes were stacked against the wall, and a long, rusted metal bar draped with clothing was suspended by coat hangers from the pipes in the ceiling.

She heard someone coming down the stairs.

A woman in a sari with a brightly-colored head covering stopped on the last stair. "I am closing in a few minutes. You need to go! I want no part of this! You said she was sick. Get her out of here! I'm trying to run a respectable business."

The man argued with her. "We are renting this storeroom."

"You said you needed space for boxes. I agreed for one month. This is not what we agreed on. You get out *now*."

The woman picked up Jessica's gun. "Or what?"

The man spoke scathingly, "You shame Muslims!"

The shop girl glared at them. "I am an American who practices the Muslim faith. You are a terrorist who uses the Muslim faith as an excuse to terrorize." She turned and stormed up the stairs, while the woman in the burqa started yelling at the man.

"Where are those idiots with the van? They should be here with the girl!"

The man shrugged not bothering to look up from the laptop. "Maybe the girl not there yet."

The woman waved her darkly draped arm toward Jessica. "And what we do with this one?"

The man glared back defiantly. "They be here soon. We will make video of her death and show Americans we are in control."

The woman stood and looked out the window. "This is taking too long. Maybe we just leave her here?"

"No! We agree everyone to go dark, remember? That way, no one trace us. They are on their way."

The woman paced under the window. "It was stupid to grab her before we had the van here."

The man stood and slapped her face, knocking her to the floor, and tearing the head covering off her niqab, the veil covering her face. "You blame me? How dare you question plan? I do everything! I had *successful* kill today! I track Emma Carr's cell phone to bar this morning. I tell you when she leave and go home. I sit in cafe two days watching people go in and out of FBI entrance. When we get opportunity like this again?"

The woman held her hand to her cheek. "You should have grabbed her at her home."

The man raised his hand to her, threatening to hit her again. "She had dog making too much noise."

Jessica's words dripped with sarcasm. "Like the dog I ran into this morning?"

Ahmed lunged at her. "I don't explain myself to you. You will pay for your disobedience."

"I've paid for it all my life. Your threats are nothing to me."

He waved his knife under his chin slowly and stared at her. "You are dead."

She glanced at the gun sitting on the box. "You sicken me. You can't touch me in America."

He snarled back. "So you think."

Jessica lay quietly, listening to their conversation. At the mention of her dog, she realized why Jeb had torn up her new blinds. He had been acting as her fierce protector, defending her apartment.

When the jackhammering outside started again, Jessica cut the tape from her feet and pulled the garrote wire free from the drawstring seam in her jacket. She reached inside a hidden pocket of her jacket and wrapped her fingers around the flat mace canister. She positioned herself with her weapons and coughed, signaling she was awake.

The guy on the floor reached for his long knife and moved toward the box. When he kicked it, Jessica faked a moan.

When he bent down to poke her awake with the knife, Jessica sprang at him with the mace, and kicked the knife out of his hand. Taking advantage of the few seconds he was disoriented, she spun him around and hooked the garrote wire around his throat, using him as a shield.

The woman in the burqa went for the gun. Jessica held the garrote wire with one hand and twisted her knife into the man's kidney with the other, shoving him at the woman. With her hands free, Jessica grabbed the mace and sprayed it into the woman's eyes, tackling her to the ground and wrestling her for the gun.

The man was grabbing at Jessica's leg, fueling her adrenaline. She struggled with the woman over control of the gun, pushing the barrel away from her and aiming it at the man. The other woman's finger was on the trigger when the gun went off, splattering his brains against the wall. Blood covered every inch of the small room.

With her legs free from the man's grip, Jessica gained more traction. She jerked the gun free and realized the woman was clawing at her burqa. She swiftly pinned the woman's arms over her head and ripped off the torn head covering.

She knew this woman's face. Where had she seen it before? Her head covering had concealed her dyed platinum blonde hair.

Something sharp was stabbing at Jessica's knee when she pinned it across the woman's stomach. She wrenched the woman's arms behind her back and bound them with the garrote wire, then pulled open the coat of her burqa, revealing a suicide belt.

Jessica spotted the woman's cell phone on the windowsill. She yanked the woman's bleeding wrists away from her body and jerked her to her feet, slamming her into the folding chair with her arms stretched painfully over the back of the chair. She reached down and peeled off the duct tape still stuck to her legs to secure the woman's arms and kicking feet to the metal chair.

Chapter 21
Playtime's over

Monday, May 9th, 9:00 p.m.

Jessica retrieved the cell phone from the windowsill and dialed 911. "Okay, bitch! Playtime's over."

"Wait! We can make deal."

Jessica paused and stared down at her. "You got a name?"

"Lana."

"Okay, Lana. Here's the deal. I'm sick of you, and you can make a *deal* with someone else."

"If you don't make the call, I'll tell you information your government wants."

The stench in the room stung Jessica's nose and throat. She wanted to shower off the man's remains and get out of there. She punched speakerphone, dialed 911, and glanced at the woman in the chair. "Uh-huh."

"911. What's your emergency?"

"This is Agent Jessica Murphy with the FBI. I have a woman wearing a bomb and one deceased male with a gunshot to the head. I'm in a storage room in the basement of a store. I think I'm around the corner from the Hoover Building. I can't move from my position to identify the address or it will compromise the bomb."

"We've got you. The owner of that shop just called in a possible gunshot from two trespassers with a possible hostage. I'm guessing that is you."

"I think so. I need a bomb squad ASAP. Can you also call Assistant Director Bill Carr?"

"Stay on the line, I'll use another line to call, since they are already on their way."

The HRT (Hostage Rescue Team) burst through the door minutes later with their weapons drawn. "HANDS IN THE AIR!"

Jessica spoke quickly, and with authority. "I'm Jessica Murphy, FBI Special Assistant to the Assistant Director of Counter Terrorism, and I can't release my hands, because I need to make sure this woman doesn't detonate her suicide belt!"

The small eight by ten room erupted in total chaos. The HRT relieved Jessica of Lana, while a bomb technician squeezed down the crowded stairway to remove the suicide belt. He unstrapped it, put it into a container, and quickly left the scene.

Jessica pressed past the SWAT, NCRT (National Capitol Rescue Team), and the Capitol Police to the outside, where the rain had slowed to a slight drizzle. She gulped in the fresh air, walked to the curb, and dropped down to sit next to the ambulance. A female EMT had been watching her since she walked out the door.

"Are you hurt?"

"I don't think so."

She handed her a roll of sanitized wet wipes and helped her wipe the blood off her face and skin, then gave her a bottle of water.

Jessica accepted the water "Thanks." She pulled at the blood-soaked clothes clinging to her skin. "I need to burn these clothes."

The EMT wrinkled her nose. "I never get used to that."

Jessica offered a middle finger wave to Lana as she was escorted out of the building with her hands handcuffed behind her back, and then buckled into the back of a black van.

A while later, the FBI Evidence Response Team (ERT) emerged from the building carrying cameras and bags of evidence. Shortly after they left, two men in uniforms carried out a body bag.

Jessica had described the events to the first responders—and again to federal agents—so many times now, it seemed like old news.

Chapter 22
The Rescue

Monday, May 9th, 7:00 p.m.

Rondie clicked on the alert to track her phone. It showed the phone was at the Kentmoor Marina on the Eastern Shore. She watched the blue dot start moving. She switched the map mode to satellite and zoomed in until she saw it traveling in a remote, area of a wooded terrain, and then it stopped. She zoomed in closer. Why had it stopped in the middle of the woods after only five minutes? She leaned back in the galley booth and sighed. "That can't be good."

She checked the taser recharging on the table. "Good to go." She reached in her little oven and filled her pockets with fresh magazines for her 9mm automatic, then did one last look around while patting her pockets. "Guns, ammo, taser, and iPad." After getting a candy bar from the refrigerator, she closed up her boat and tucked her iPad under her raincoat.

She pulled up the bright yellow hood and tiptoed past the crime scene to the slip owners' parking lot, noting that Blake's car had been towed away. A young police officer smiled at her as one would their grandmother. "Be careful, ma'am, it's slick."

Rondie mentally rolled her eyes and pasted on her best impression of a grandmotherly smile while she walked to her car. She laid her iPad on the console, opened her candy bar, and drove toward the Eastern Shore with heavy metal blasting on the radio.

An hour and a half later, it was dark when she parked in the middle of a country road in the drizzling rain. The app showed she had reached her destination, but she didn't see any sign of Karen. She fished a long-handled maglight out of her glove box and squinted into the woods. Nothing.

She flicked the safety off the gun in her holster and the taser, pulled her shotgun from under the seat, tugged up her hood and stepped outside. She walked along the road approaching an old bridge when she saw a huge buck charging toward her. She raised her shotgun and caught it right between the eyes. An eight-point buck. As she shone her floodlight on it, she noticed it was already wounded—blood was running down its legs and sides.

Tire tracks led off to the ditch behind it. She spotted something shiny under some trees, and cautiously gauged her footing while she half-scooted down the steep embankment. She stopped when she thought she heard someone talking. She snugged her shotgun to her shoulder and aimed toward the voices.

Karen froze with fear. "That was a gunshot!"

Liam pierced her with a serious stare. "Stay calm. I'm going to climb through the sunroof and see what's going on."

Karen threw her hands in the air. "You can't even sit up, let alone climb up there." She inhaled deeply, summoning her courage. "I'll go up."

"No. Stay put."

Karen snapped. "Are you seriously still trying to tell me what to do? You're not in any position to do that."

Thundering noise on top of the SUV and falling debris stopped their argument.

Rondie stared down into the sunroof. "Hey, I came to get my phone."

Karen almost wept with relief. "Rondie! How did you find me?"

"The tracker app on my phone."

Liam glared at Karen menacingly.

Karen rolled her neck in defiance and held up her pointer finger. "Don't. Even. Say it. That phone just saved your ass!"

Rondie interrupted Karen's rant. "We gotta get out of here. You've got water rising up to the wheels, and if I can track you, so can someone else. Karen, give me your hand."

Karen reached up and winced. "I think I've broken a rib."

"You wouldn't be able to do so much talking. You're fine. Push through the pain and climb out."

Karen stopped and dragged her BOB bag up on the seat. She hoisted the bag over her head to Rondie and cried out in pain.

Rondie closed the safety, placed the shotgun on the SUV hood and reached for the bag. "What's this?"

"My survival kit."

Rondie hoisted it over her shoulder and pulled on Karen's arms. Pain seared through the torn flesh on Karen's knees when she hit the top of the SUV, and she cried out again. She quickly rolled over into a sitting position, panting to catch her breath.

Rondie frowned down at Liam's dislocated shoulder. "You don't look so good." She climbed through the sunroof to where Liam was holding his arm. She felt the mushy socket. "It's definitely out. I can try to put it back; it'll make it easier to get you out."

Liam nodded. "Do it."

"Scoot over to the door as close as you can." She fastened the seat belt tight around him and placed her feet against his hip and her back against the passenger door. "Relax as best you can. I'm going to pull on your arm and ease it back into the socket."

Liam nodded.

Rondie braced her feet against Liam's hip to provide the counter tension she needed to stretch the muscles around the ball. She gently pulled on his arm. "You're doing good. The muscles are still stretching. That's a good sign."

Liam gritted his teeth and stifled a scream.

Rondie pulled with all her weight and felt the muscles pull the ball back into the socket. "Good job! Can you touch your other shoulder?"

Liam had felt his shoulder pop back into place. He reached over and touched his opposite shoulder. "You got it!" He looked down at his ankle, which was so swollen there was no definition between his calf and foot. "How are you with a sprained ankle?"

"Can you put pressure on it?"

Liam bore down and winced. "Sort of. It'll be fine." He pushed the seat back as far as it would go and raised the steering wheel. "You go ahead and climb out."

Rondie shook her head. "No, it'll be easier if I push you rather than pull."

Karen poked her head through the roof. "What do you want me to do?"

"Slip your arms under his armpits and pull him up. Careful of his shoulder. I'll push."

Liam held his palms out. "I've got this." He was able to use both arms and push with his good foot until he was kneeling in the seat.

From there the three of them pushed, pulled and rolled their way free of the SUV and crawled back up the embankment. When they reached the top, three men dressed in camouflage and holding knives were standing outside their truck by the deer.

Karen froze, and Rondie slowly reached over her shoulder for her shotgun. "Hello."

The three men were startled to see them. "Hey, this your deer?"

"Yeah. It forced my friend's car off the road and down the embankment."

"Wow! That's too bad. You want this deer?"

Rondie released her grip on the gun and shook her head. "No, it's yours if you want it."

They bent over the deer and slit its throat. "Thanks, ma'am. You want us to call for help or somethin'?"

Liam waved his hand as he limped toward the car. "No, we're fine. I called a tow, and we've got a ride."

Karen limped over to the backseat of Rondie's car and winced when she saw the knees of her sweatpants were soaked with blood. Liam and Rondie climbed in front. They waved at the three hunters while they pulled away.

Liam saw the time on the dash. 9:10 p.m. "I was supposed to meet the Assistant Director at the Easton Airport by now, and you were supposed to check in at the TSL over an hour ago."

Chapter 23
Lawyered Up

Monday, May 9, 5:30 p.m.

Cal was completely confused when Rondie and Larry confronted him at the bar and told him they needed to question him about his involvement in a murder. He assumed it was a case of mistaken identity until he walked to the front of the restaurant and saw Lana's two friends on the ground in handcuffs. He had been suspicious of them for a while. He found it odd they never came around when he was home, and it didn't make sense that they were always picking her up for job interviews.

His stomach dropped when the agents asked him if he knew them. It was the first time he'd ever questioned what Lana was involved in.

He sat in silence on the way to the Annapolis FBI office, thinking about who to call. He didn't have the money for an attorney, nor did he know any. He was left with no other choice but to call his parents.

His hand was shaking as he dialed his parents' number. He knew they were already disappointed in him for avoiding their calls over the past few weeks, ever since Lana had arrived. His mouth was dry when his mother answered.

"Hello?"

"Mom, I don't have much time to talk. I'm at the FBI headquarters in Annapolis. They've brought me in for questioning for my involvement in an attempted murder. Could you call a criminal lawyer for me?"

"What? What are you talking about? Why would they think you were involved in a murder? Who do they believe you were trying to murder?"

"They think I was involved in a plot against Emma Carr. Mom, I can't talk. Would you *please* hire a lawyer and send him to the Annapolis FBI office?"

Cal's father came on the line. "Cal, what is this all about? Why is your mother crying?"

"Dad, I'm running out of time. I had nothing to do with what they are accusing me of, but I'm involved with a girl who probably is. I need a criminal lawyer. I'm at the Annapolis FBI office. Could you please call a criminal lawyer for me?"

"Sit tight, son. We'll be there. And I'll call around first and find you a criminal lawyer."

An hour later, Cal was sitting across from the lawyer his parents had sent, consumed with shame. How could he have been so stupid?

The small conference room smelled of body odor and stale air. Cal wiped his sweaty hands on his jeans and crossed his arms.

His lawyer introduced himself and pulled a notepad and pen from his satchel. "Let's go over this from the beginning. You were talking to a Syrian girl online, and then she showed up at your door?"

"Yes."

"How did she get here?"

"She told me she came over on a thirty-day visitor's visa, and that she could stay for a year if she found work and a place to stay. I let her live with me, and offered to help her find a job, but she kept insisting she had people here helping her find work."

"Did you ever meet any of these people?"

Cal dropped his eyes to his folded hands. "Yes. The two guys at the marina picked her up at my house a couple of times."

His lawyer nodded and took notes. As Cal told the story for the first time out loud, he could see how he'd been used. His blood pressure and emotions skyrocketed back and forth between anger and heartbreak.

"How long has she been here?"

"About a month."

"How long had you been writing to each other?"

"Almost two years."

"Okay, what happened from the time she showed up at the house until now?"

Cal rubbed at the fingerprint ink on his fingers, remembering how he and Lana made love, soaked in the bath, laughed, went out to dinner, ate carryout in bed, visited DC tourist spots, walked through Georgetown, and together experienced the best of life.

He covered his mouth with his fist and cleared his throat, suppressing his hurt, regret and shame. "It was great. She wanted to learn everything about America. She seemed happy to be here."

He sipped his water for a diversion from his anguish. The pain of her deception felt like heavy weights on his chest.

His lawyer tapped his pen and leaned back. "Why was today different? Did you have any idea she was a radicalized Muslim?"

Cal winced at the reference. "No. I never heard or saw her practice her religion. It never came up."

"What did you talk about?"

Cal thought back over the many discussions they'd had. "Our feelings for each other. Our future. Movies. Art, she loved art. She read a lot. She'd never read or heard of the New York Times Best Sellers list. She was consumed with those books, and constantly recharging my Kindle from hours of reading. She had such a thirst for life."

The lawyer nodded. "So, what happened this morning?"

Cal shrugged and threw up his palms dejectedly. "She got up and went out for a run. On her way out, she said she'd meet me later in the afternoon, because she was meeting with friends about a job."

"Why were you at The Tombs today?"

"Lana called and asked if I'd meet her there for lunch. I had been watching the door for her for a while. Emma Carr was sitting between the door and me. She waved, and I acknowledged her with a nod at the same time Lana came in. Lana saw the exchange when she entered the bar, asked who Emma was, and I told her."

"What did Lana do then?"

Cal's eyebrows pinched together in deep thought. "She kind of got all fidgety and asked if I wanted to leave. I thought maybe she was jealous of Emma."

"Why were you at the marina?"

Cal exhaled loudly. "Lana called earlier and told me her friends had car trouble and asked me if I could pick them up at the marina. I'd been waiting and reading the news about Emma on my phone when she came around the corner. I was shocked when I saw her there."

"Why did you leave and go into the restaurant when you saw her?"

"I was on my way in when I saw her. I was looking for the two guys I was supposed to meet, and tired of standing out in the rain. I thought maybe they'd be at the bar."

His lawyer leaned forward and frowned. "Do you hear how coincidental this all sounds?"

"I swear, I am telling you the truth."

"Federal agents are searching your apartment. What are they going to find?"

"They'll see all her stuff—clothes and toiletries. I don't know that she has much other than her cell phone, and I'm sure she has that with her. She always carried around a backpack with her stuff."

"Okay. What can you tell me about her?"

Cal took a deep breath and exhaled slowly. "When we used to chat online, she was sweet and funny. At first, I would correct her English and explain what different phrases meant. She caught on quickly, and was extremely curious about America and my life. It was nice to have someone so interested in me. She was so appreciative of anything I did for her. She reacted like a little kid to the simplest things. She had led a very sheltered life."

His lawyer took off his jacket and hung it on the back of his chair. "Did anyone else meet this girl? Your parents? Friends?"

"No. She was very shy about meeting my parents and friends."

"What about the two other guys at the marina? What can you tell me about them?"

"Not much. They were her friends. I saw them one day when they came by my house to pick her up for an interview, and then again today at the marina."

"Those two murdered Emma's boyfriend and tried to abduct her. They may also be linked to the murder of a military family earlier today."

Cal ran his fingers through his hair with desperation. "I swear I don't have any connections with them."

The lawyer raised his brows, and his eyes softened. "Are there any phone records connecting you to them?"

Cal shook his head. "I have never called them. If there are any phone calls, I didn't make them."

His lawyer cleared his throat and flipped the page in his notebook. "Agents are at your parents' house, too. Will they turn up anything there?"

Cal shook his head and knotted his hands into tight fists, inhaling deeply to maintain control over his emotions. They had given him everything. They were so proud of him. How could he do this to them? He cleared his throat and took a sip of water. "When can I talk to my parents?"

"They're outside. We can meet them in another room, but you need to know anything you say in their presence will be recorded. The FBI will be listening."

Cal blinked back his stinging tears and bit his trembling lip. "I am telling you the truth. I had no idea what she was doing."

"I believe you, but you need to be careful not to incriminate yourself. I'll stop you if I feel you are wandering into suspicious territory, and you have to change the subject immediately. Agreed?"

Cal nodded. They left the small room and entered a bigger room with a large two-way mirror. Cal's mother, Peggy, burst into tears and threw her arms around him. His father stood back and asked, "What is this all about, Cal?"

Chapter 24
Bill's relief

Monday, May 9th, 9:05 p.m.

Bill's secretary knocked at the door before she left to go home, pulling him from his frantic thoughts and accusations. "Sir, a DC Metro dispatcher is on the line. They say they received a 911 caller instructing them to call you. The caller's name is Jessica."

Bill picked up the phone on his desk. "This is Assistant Director Bill Carr."

"We received a 911 call from a woman claiming to be your assistant. She has a woman with a suicide belt. We still have her on the line and are sending out bomb technicians."

"Where is she?"

The dispatcher gave Bill the address, and he called the Washington FBI field office to talk to his friend Gary, who was with the NCRT (National Capitol Response Team).

"Gary? Bill Carr. What can you tell me about the woman with the suicide belt Jessica is holding?"

"It's under a small retail shop. My guys are there now. At this point, all I know is that there is one deceased male from a gunshot wound to the head, and your agent is restraining a female with a suicide belt."

"Okay, Gary, thanks. Can you call me directly with any updates?"

"Sure thing, Bill."

Bill had barely hung up the phone when Agent Marcs appeared at his door. "Sir, Agent Murphy's phone was turned in across the street at the sandwich shop. Someone found it in the gutter across from the Indian dress shop."

Bill frowned at Agent Marcs. "I just got a call from the 911 dispatcher telling me Jessica is in the basement of that shop with a woman wrapped in a suicide belt."

Agent Marcs eyes popped wide. "What?!"

Bill nodded and rubbed his hand over his face. "She's in a basement storage room. Get over there and let me know what the hell is going on."

Agent Marcs turned and flew out of the room. "Yes, sir."

***

Agent Marcs double-parked his black SUV when he spied Jessica, who was covered in blood and sitting on the curb next to the ambulance. The area had been sealed off with yellow crime tape, and the DC Police were securing the perimeter. He flashed his badge and ducked under the tape.

"Jessica."

Jessica turned toward the familiar voice. She grinned, took a sip from her bottle of water, and asked casually. "So, how's it going?"

Agent Marcs returned her grin with his hands in his pockets. "Good." He pointed at Jessica's shirt. "Looks like you got something on your shirt."

Jessica looked down at her shirt and pretended to brush away the blood covering her clothes. "Well, crap. That's probably going to stain."

"Bummer."

"Yeah, it was one of my favorites."

"Well, Bill sent me over here to see what you've been up to."

"Not much, really. I was on my way to get some sleep when I was drugged, dragged down some stairs, stuffed in a box soaked with cat piss, and splattered with some guy's brains when a crazy bitch shot him instead of me."

"Cat piss, huh? That sucks."

Someone yelled from the door. "Agent Murphy, you've been cleared to leave."

Jessica tilted her head at Agent Marcs. "Looks like I need a ride."

He raised his brows and scanned her head to toe. "Seriously?"

The EMT reached into the ambulance and grabbed a clear plastic tarp. "Here, this will help."

Agent Marcs caught the tarp the EMT tossed at him and asked, "Got any air freshener we could hang around her neck?"

The EMT busted out laughing while Jessica tried to stifle her smile.

Marcs spread the plastic sheet over the seat, and Jessica climbed in the car very carefully.

Once he was behind the wheel, Marcs looked at her and asked, "Where to?"

"I'm exhausted. Do you think I can go home?"

"Your TSL is just a few minutes away, and I think you should still have the security. I heard from the guys at the command center that it's real swanky."

Jessica yawned, her eyes heavy. "Talked me into it."

Marcs fished Jessica's phone out of his jacket. "Here, someone turned this in to the sandwich shop. They found it in the gutter outside."

Jessica scrolled through the missed calls and messages and turned off the phone. "Tell Bill what happened, and that I'll turn this phone back on after I've gotten some sleep."

Marcs pulled into the underground garage and stopped at the elevator leading up to the apartments. "You got the code for the elevator?"

She climbed out of the car and wadded up the plastic sheet. "Yeah, I'm good. I'll talk to you later. Thanks for the ride."

Marcs flipped his hand in a wave. "You got it." He watched her get into the elevator before pulling out of the garage.

***

Bill's phone rang, showing blocked caller. He answered reluctantly, "Carr."

"Sir, this is Agent Garrison."

Bill controlled his temper. He wanted to reach through the phone and rip out Garrison's throat for making him worry for so long. He spoke in a low monotone. "Where the hell are you?"

"We are en route to the medical center. A deer hit our vehicle and sent us down an embankment."

Bill's anger switched quickly to worry. "Is anyone hurt? Can I talk to Karen?"

"Yes, sir." Liam handed the phone back to Karen.

"Bill?"

Bill broke into a sweat with relief. "Oh, God, Karen. Are you all right?"

"I think so. My knees are banged up, but Liam is looking worse. Rondie popped his shoulder back in place, but his ankle is in bad shape, and he'll need stitches in his head. He needs to go to the hospital."

Bill was confused. "Did you say Rondie?"

"Yes. She gave me her phone when I left the pier, and used it to track us down when she saw it stopped moving."

"What?"

"Oh, Bill, this is too complicated to get into over the phone. What do you want us to do?"

Bill's head was swimming from lack of sleep and the shocking events that had erupted in the last fifteen minutes. "The medical center closed at seven-thirty. You'll have to go to the hospital emergency room. I'll take care of security." Bill closed his eyes tightly and swallowed. "Karen, I love you."

Karen heard the raw, heartfelt emotion in his voice. Her eyes flooded with tears, and in a hoarse whisper said, "I love you, too."

Bill hung up the phone and realized he'd told his secretary to go home, and his Special Assistant was in a basement somewhere holding onto a woman in a suicide belt. He tasked the Staff Operations Assistant to make the necessary calls for the security arrangements at the hospital.

When they pulled up to the hospital, security greeted them, and within ten minutes an FBI agent from the Eastern Shore arrived. Rondie went into full leadership mode, ordering the doctors, nurses, agents, and security in place, essentially telling everyone what to do, and how to do it.

Karen was stitched up quickly and escorted by Agent Dutton back to Rondie in a private waiting room. "Where's Liam?"

Rondie pointed at the door. "He's in there. No one has come out. I think it's more serious than we thought."

Agent Dutton cleared his throat. "We need to report in to the Assistant Director. My orders were to take Mrs. Carr into DC."

Rondie raised her brows. "Are you kidding?"

"No. The threat has been contained. There is an apartment set up for the family to use for the next few days."

Karen sighed, closed her eyes, and rested her head back against the wall. "I just want to go home, shower, and crawl into my own bed, and have my daughter tucked into her own bed in the next room."

Rondie stood and walked to the door. "I'll be back in a minute." She stepped outside and made a few calls. When she stepped back into the waiting room twenty minutes later, Liam was sitting on the vinyl couch with crutches and a partially shaved head with bandaged stitches.

Everyone looked up expectantly when she walked back into the room.

Karen spoke up, "Well? What did you find out?"

"Suspected sleeper cell. Two ISIL—a male and a female, and two radicalized Americans. The female was Cal's *pen pal*. His involvement is questionable. They somehow got hold of the list of names and took it upon themselves to assassinate each and every one they could get to."

Karen nearly fell out of her chair. "What?! Peggy's Cal? I've watched him grow up. You are telling me he was writing to a terrorist?"

Rondie nodded.

"How long?"

Rondie put her finger across her lips. "Shhh." She spoke in a hushed tone to keep Karen from freaking out again. "A couple of years. He claims he had no idea."

"Oh, my gosh. This is why Peggy was so upset with me when I called her earlier. She thinks *Emma* did something." Karen's brows pinched from worry and she stared at Rondie. "She didn't, did she?"

Rondie shook her head and smiled. "No. Emma is an innocent victim in all of this." She hesitated and fidgeted with her phone. "Have you heard what happened?"

Karen shook her head, not sure she was ready to hear what Rondie would say.

"Blake is dead. The two radicalized Americans murdered him." Rondie dragged her pointed finger across her neck. "Slit his throat."

Karen flew out of her chair and gasped. "Oh, my God! His poor parents…and Emma…oh, my God." Karen's hands were shaking, and tears burned her eyes.

"Blake went back to Emma's apartment with her, and two men were waiting for them. Blake ran after one and was killed. The other grabbed Emma, but she got away and fled to the boat."

Karen gasped and her hand flew over her heart.

Rondie continued, "That's when she and I went looking for you in my boat. The storm forced us back to the pier, and they tried to grab Emma again. There were agents in place who secured Emma and took the rest into custody. Cal was there, and was taken in for questioning."

Karen sat back down, shaking her head. "I can't believe what you are telling me. Emma must have been scared out of her mind."

"She did fine," answered Rondie.

Karen threw up her hands. "I've known that boy for ten years. They live next door."

"Cal says he didn't know. She's been living with him for the past month, though. It doesn't look good. He's going to need a good lawyer."

Liam could barely stay awake after the painkillers he'd been given. He had insisted he would be fine to go home. He forced himself to stay awake and listen to Karen and Rondie.

Silence fell over the room.

Agent Dutton broke the quiet. "I think we need to go. Agent Garrison, I can drop you home after I deliver Mrs. Carr to the new TSL for the Assistant Director in DC."

Liam rolled his head in the agent's direction and slurred, "Suure, that's great." He slowly rolled his head back to Rondie and dropped his chin, causing his head to bob. He pointed his finger at her and tried to keep his words together. "But firsht, I wanna know how you got that information."

Rondie pulled her car keys from her pocket. "I know people." She walked to the door and waved goodbye. "It's been real, folks. Take care."

Chapter 25
The Barn

Monday, May 9th, 9:20 p.m.

A special operation force consisting of four Counterterrorism special agents, an attorney from the Department of Justice, and a translator for Lana were gathered around a table in the bland-colored conference room. They were discussing the interrogation of each member of the sleeper cell, and what intelligence they planned to collect from each, when Lana appeared on the other side of the two-way mirror.

Two of the Counterterrorism special agents and the translator left to join her in the interrogation room. Lana was sitting handcuffed in a chair. She appeared calm and smiled at the agents when they sat across from her and turned on a tape recorder.

"You will make this much easier on yourself if you cooperate. Do you understand what I'm saying to you?"

Lana nodded.

The agent waved his hand toward the translator. "This is a translator in case you would like our questions translated for clarification."

"Not necessary."

"How did you come into the United States?"

"Through Mexico. I paid guards, and we traveled through drug cartel tunnel. We paid more guards, and they loaded us into a truck to take us to where we met our friend in California."

"Where is this tunnel?"

"I have not been there before, so I cannot tell you. I only see the tunnel after the truck ride. I went through the tunnel, and got into another truck.

Lana enjoyed the interrogation. She was treated with respect, and could tell that what she said to them mattered. She sat at a table and answered truthfully about everything they wanted to know. She had disposed of her burqa and switched to her American personality, wearing the tight jeans and T-shirt she had on earlier at the café.

"How did you get from California to DC?"

"We rode in trucks. Electricity trucks. No one stops a utility truck."

"What were your instructions? Are there more of you?"

"Many more, all over the United States. After America started bombing our camps, we were told to make American friends on the Internet and wage jihad in America. Some go through Canada, but many carry drugs through Mexico. It's much easier for them to travel with a woman or child. Not so many checks or questions for women. I had one month to prove I can make a difference, or they will use me for suicide bomb. If they do not think I am dead, they will come after me.

"Our instructions are to kill infidels. All my life, I'm told to hate Americans because they plot to kill followers of Islam, and they are the Great Satan. But when I get here, no one cares or asks what religion I am. It's not important what your faith is. Very confusing to me at first. But peaceful. No violence or bombings. I can walk to movie or restaurant at night by myself. No curfew. Beautiful parks and buildings. I can take off my burqa, and people see me as a person. They smile and talk to me. It is so freeing. I never had it before.

"Where are the others?"

"We were told to go dark when we got to America. We were not to communicate unless by *friends*."

"Who are these friends?"

"Americans who want to join ISIL. Your government doesn't watch Americans. They talk to other friends and pass information. Ahmed kept track of the friends."

The agents exchanged a quick glance. They knew the man called Ahmed's laptop and cell phone had been confiscated and were being analyzed.

"Were you involved with the murder of that family this morning?"

Lana hesitated. Technically, she wasn't. "No."

The interrogator frowned. "Do you know who was?"

Lana nodded.

"Who was it?"

"Ahmed. The man who died today in the basement."

"Why did he do it?"

"American jihad. To kill infidels. It's important they know what it feels like to lose your whole family in war. They are killing our families in Syria."

"Why that family?"

"I got a list of soldier names who are in Syria killing our people."

"What if I told you it was a list of soldiers who were there to help the Syrian people? To make sure needed supplies were guarded, so innocent women and children could survive?"

Lana's head snapped up, and her eyes were wide. "Is that true?"

"We're trying to bring peace to that area."

Lana's ISIL personality was triggered, and she sneered. "By bombing us? You kill my father in the streets and murdered my mother while I was still holding her hand. No. You are not innocent like you pretend."

"Where did you get the list with the names?"

"A guy on Facebook who worked for the FBI. I friended him and talked to him. Sent him my picture. He thinks I am his girlfriend. I asked him to prove to me he work for FBI. One day we meet and walk around DC. He showed me on his phone a list he said was top secret. He said he worked on important cases. He left his phone on the table, and I took a picture of his list with my phone and gave it to Ahmed. Ahmed matched the names on list to names and addresses from the government files that were hacked, and matched names to addresses near here, then we pledged their deaths to ISIL.

"What is his name?"

Lana sighed and cut her eyes to the side. "I don't remember."

The agent slid an iPad across the table. "Can you sign onto your Facebook and show me the man you met who said he worked for the FBI?"

Lana accepted the iPad and signed in awkwardly, with the handcuffs limiting her movements. She searched for the conversation, scrolling through her posts. "It's not here." She tried to look for his page. "He is not here anymore."

The agent wrote a few notes and nodded.

"I'm telling you the truth!"

"How many are in your cell?"

"It *was* Ahmed, who is dead, and two Americans. One American I meet in Syria. His cousin convinced him to join us when he was there to be with his grandparents. He came back here to his mosque and brought other one to us. I met him when I get here."

"What about Cal?"

She looked down at her folded hands. "He doesn't know who I really am. He believes I am here on visitor visa and looking for job."

"What can you tell me about the two Americans?"

"Ahmed talked to them before we came over. They were his friends. He mostly recruited them. He trained one in Syria; the other he trained when he met him here. But before that, the other one watched our videos."

***

In the other rooms, the agents heard very different stories from the two male prisoners.

The agent entered the room with the older of the two Americans. One arm was in a sling from the shoulder wound, and the other hand was handcuffed to the bar bolted to the middle of the table.

The agent wore a pair of khaki dress pants and a blue striped shirt. He sat on the opposite side of the table and tapped his pen on a pad of paper. "What's your name?"

"Yousef." He avoided eye contact and scowled.

"Okay, Yousef. Do you have a last name?"

Yousef shook a head full of shoulder-length black curls. His beard was patchy and scruffy-looking.

The agent continued in a calm monotone. "How old are you?"

"Nineteen."

"Where are your parents?"

"My family is Syrian."

"You speak very good English, with an East Coast accent. Where do your parents live?"

Yousef stuck his chin in the air with arrogance. "I have nothing to do with my parents. They have sold out to America."

"Are you saying your parents are Americans?"

"Yes. They are legal immigrants from Syria. They turned their backs on our people."

"Do they know what you are involved in?"

"They know nothing. They came here as refugees, and pretended to maintain close contacts with our family members still in Syria and Iraq, but they sold out."

"Did you go to school here?"

Yousef had a sarcastic edge in his voice. "Yes, I graduated from high school."

"Do you have a job?"

"No. I am a soldier."

"Are you a paid soldier? Where do you live?"

Yousef stared into the agent's eyes. "Yes. I am paid very well."

The agent leaned forward and narrowed his eyes. "Son, maybe you don't understand how serious this is. You are charged with murdering a young man, attempted murder of a young woman, and conspiracy to commit the murders of a military family. You are looking at life in prison at best."

Yousef closed his eyes. *"Allahu akbar."*

The agent glanced up at the camera disgustedly. The agents behind the two-way mirror suggested another line of questioning via his earpiece. They gave him information from the other suspect's interview.

"We found your laptop in the van." He pulled out a picture of Yousef in camouflage holding an AK-47 under a jihad banner. "Where was this taken?"

Yousef's eyes narrowed with anger. "You don't know anything."

The agent pulled other papers from the brown file folder and started reading emails from his Syrian cousin, who had been responsible for radicalizing him, and a series of Dear John letters from his ex-girlfriend.

Yousef was seething while he listened to his personal email being read aloud. He clenched his jaw and ground his teeth. "Shut up!"

The agent leaned back in his chair and propped his ankle over his other knee. "Looks to me like you went over to visit Grandma after high school when your girlfriend dumped you. Mommy and Daddy thought you were visiting the homeland to learn about your culture, but your cousin had a more radical view of your culture."

The agent leaned forward and continued to taunt him. "Did you think ISIL was going to be an adventure? Did your *comrades* make you feel important? Did they feed you all the bullshit about building a new society and promising you paradise with seventy-three virgins? It's all lies!"

Yousef exploded, spouting all the propaganda they'd fed him. "I am important. I was *chosen* to wage jihad in America! We will avenge our homelands."

***

In the other room, the American with the knee wound was telling another version of their story.

Agent Price strode in wearing black tactical gear and sat on the corner of the table in close proximity to Muhammad. He smacked the brown file folder on the table and folded his arms.

"Your friend has given us quite a lot of information on you already. This will go much easier on you if you cooperate at this point. First, what is your name?"

Sweat dripped from the prisoner's hairline, and his swollen toes ached from the bandages around his knee. "Muhammad Abdul."

"Where do you live?"

"I've been living with Yousef since I was kicked out of my parents' house."

"Why were you kicked out of your parents' house?"

Muhammad shrugged, looking down at his hands.

The agent opened the file and read from one of the papers. "Runaway. Gang activity. Arrest record. Did this have anything to do with it?"

"My parents didn't understand. They are grateful for American handouts, and expect me to live that way. Their home in Iraq was bombed, and they were beaten before they came here as refugees. They are satisfied to grovel for a meager existence. I am not. I was born an American, but because of them, everyone sees me as a foreigner, and treats me like a second-class citizen.

"I wasn't part of a gang. All our parents were Iraqi, and we hung out together to protect each other's backs. The kids in our high school thought they could kick us around until we decided not to take it anymore."

"What do you call that if it's not a gang?"

Muhammad scowled. "It was to protect ourselves! You don't understand."

The agent thumbed through the file and read another sheet. "Armed robbery. Attempted murder."

Muhammad slammed his fist down on the table, causing the handcuffs to bite into his wrist. "I was taking back what was mine! He stole my bike and my little sister's iPod."

Agent Price's voice softened. "When did you meet Yousef?"

"A year or so ago."

"How did you meet him?"

"At the mosque. He was there to recruit guys for the cause until they found out and banned him."

"How did you get hooked up with him?"

Muhammad took in a deep breath and exhaled slowly. "After I quit school, my parents kicked me out and told me to get a job. I couldn't find any work. I was living on the streets when I remembered Yousef had an apartment. I went there, and he took me in. He understood me. We watched videos about building a new caliphate. The Islamic State will be a paradise when we join together on the battlefield for religious glory. We are building a new society. One that is better, more meaningful. Yousef is my friend. He is an important soldier, who was especially chosen to lead us in America."

Price patted Muhammad on the shoulder. "Do you want some water?"

Muhammad nodded, staring at his hands.

The agent left the room and joined the others behind the two-way mirror.

Chapter 26
Jessica's TSL

Monday, May 9th, 10:00 p.m.

Jessica rode the elevator to the top floor and stepped off the elevator to a marble-floored foyer with dark gray-blue walls. A female agent was sitting in front of a set of thick double doors.

The agent stood and approached Jessica. "Agent Murphy?"

"Yes."

She opened the door for Jessica and escorted her into a stylish apartment. "You should have everything you need. The refrigerator is stocked, and there are toiletries in the bathroom. If you need anything, I'll be out here."

Jessica noted the fruit basket on the kitchen counter and walked straight for the bathroom. She peeled her sticky clothes off and stuffed them into the plastic bag lining the garbage can. She twisted the plastic in a knot and turned on the shower.

The hot water was transcending. It allowed her to temporarily forget the day's horrors and concentrate on the hot water pouring through her hair and over her skin. She stood under the warm spray, collecting her thoughts. After a while, she opened her eyes, washed the filth from her hair, and rinsed the rest of her day down the drain.

When she stepped out of the hot shower it was, once again, hard to find quiet in the chaos of her mind. One thought was shouting for attention, but getting drowned by the screaming competition. A memory kept gnawing at the edges of her subconscious while she towel-dried her hair. What was it she thought of earlier?

She picked up the new comb and brush set sealed in plastic next to the sink and tore the comb free from the plastic. She reached for the robe hung on the bathroom door, cinching it tightly around her, and stared into the mirror while she combed through her hair trying to organize her thoughts.

Wrapping her wet hair in a towel, she went to the refrigerator and opened it. She smiled at the Reuben sitting on the top shelf. "Someone has done their homework."

She twitched on the TV with the remote to break the silence in the apartment. Maybe it would help drown out the ringing in her ears from the gunshots fired in the tiny space this afternoon.

She bit into her sandwich and tried to suppress the mental noise from the earlier panic and confusion. She focused on a commercial with a seductive blonde advertising a new pill for erectile dysfunction—and almost choked when she suddenly knew who had leaked the file.

She checked the time and did the math. She had been awake for forty straight hours, so she jotted down her thoughts on the courtesy pad of paper and finished her sandwich. She would sleep on the idea and bounce it off Bill first chance she got.

She ripped open the packages with a new T-shirt and underwear on the dresser and put them on. She groaned when she slipped into the soft, clean sheets and fell asleep the second her head hit the pillow.

Chapter 27
Turned

Monday, May 9th, 9:30 p.m.

The special operation team sat around the conference table and stared at the bulletin board covered with the events from the past twenty-four hours.

The lead agent in charge, Agent Peterson, sat at the head of the table with a brown file folder in front of him. "Where are we with the interrogations?"

"The girl seems eager to share. She doesn't want to go back to Syria."

"What about the others?"

"My guy thinks he is a big important soldier chosen by Allah. He will need more convincing before he'll talk."

Agent Price, who interviewed Muhammad, let out a heavy sigh. "Mine is a misguided kid who was on the streets with nowhere to go. He has been brainwashed by Yousef, but…" The agent pulled at his ear and shook his head. "He's just a kid who was bullied and now has a chance to play the bully. A screwed-up kid who has been fed a load of crap and believed it because he doesn't have anything else to believe in."

Agent Peterson opened his file. "These were lifted off Ahmed's computer. It's a list of names we think are possible members of other cells. Since the girl is the most willing, go back and ask her about these names. Take her a sandwich or something for goodwill."

***

Lana smiled up at Agent Barry when he entered the room.

He sat across from her and placed the sandwich on the table. "Sandwich?"

Lana nodded and held up her handcuffs. "Please."

The agent unlocked her cuffs and shoved the piece of paper with the names next to the sandwich. "Do you recognize the names on this list?" He watched her scroll nonchalantly through the list of names while she unwrapped her sandwich.

She took a bite and picked up the paper. "Sure."

Agent Barry's brows arched revealing his surprise. "Who are they?"

"Not who. They are schools." Lana took another bite and washed it down with a sip of water. "They are targets."

The agent leaned in and folded his hands on the table. "What kind of targets?"

"If I tell you, will you help me?"

"Help you what?"

"Stay in America. I can help you. I will tell you information. I will help you find other jihadists, if you let me stay here, and make them believe I am dead."

The agent leaned forward in his chair, propped his elbows on the table and rested his chin on his folded hands. "What kind of targets? I can't promise you anything until I verify that what you are telling me is the truth. If you can give me some valuable information now, then we can talk about you staying later."

Lana stared at the agent and chewed her sandwich. She placed it on the wrapper and leaned back in her chair. "Watkins, Eaton, Shepard, all of these, they are a list of elementary schools around here. They have pipe bombs stuffed in the hollow structures of the playground equipment."

The shock on the agent's face was hard to hide. "What? Where?" He closed his eyes and shook his head to focus on his next questions.

"We are going to set them all off at one time."

Agent Peterson jumped out of his seat from behind the two-way mirror. "Jesus!" He barked questions into Agent Barry's earpiece. "Ask her when? Who has the detonator?"

Agent Barry pulled at his earpiece to limit its volume. "When were you planning to do that, and how?"

Peterson was frantically pacing behind the two-way mirror, debating whether to call 911 and report a bomb threat.

"Ahmed took care of that. He gave us orders every morning."

"Did he give Yousef orders too?"

"Yousef gave him information, and they planned together."

"What kind of information?"

"Mostly easy targets that would do the most damage."

"What other targets are there?"

"Many. They discussed parks, bridges, tunnels."

"How do I know you are telling me the truth?"

"I can show you. I put them there. That was my job for the last month."

"You just walked around town and put bombs everywhere?"

"Yes. I use stroller and backpack. No one even looked at me. They just smiled and told me how cute my baby was."

"What baby?"

"I babysit *friend's* children for covers. I'm good at this. I can work for you."

"What about *your* country?"

"ISIL is not a country. They have done nothing for me. I owe them nothing. Women are treated worse than animals. We are nothing over there. There is nothing for women like me to aspire to there. I can do something here."

Agent Peterson was shouting into Agent Barry's earpiece. "Get her to write down all addresses known to have bombs! Get descriptions. Find out who made the bombs, and how they were going to detonate them."

Agent Barry shoved the pad of paper over to Lana. "Can you write down the addresses?"

"I don't know the address. I mostly placed the bombs in school playgrounds. I didn't pay any attention to where we went. My job was to place the bombs."

"What did the bombs look like?"

"They were small white plastic pipes."

"Where on the playground?"

"Mostly in benches. The bolts were already loosened when I took off the cap and slipped the plastic pipes into the structure."

"You did this in broad daylight?"

"No, at night. I would scout out the playgrounds during the day."

"How many schools?"

"I probably placed a half dozen or so. I don't know about the others."

"Who made the bombs?"

"They bought them."

"What parks and tunnels?"

"One is outside the Botanical Gardens by the water garden next to the little stage. I'm not sure about the tunnels. They couldn't get to them. They are routinely swept for bombs, and the security video is too much. It may just be the schools and the Botanical Gardens."

"What about the bridges?"

"I'm not sure. I know they are talking to homeless men who live under them."

"Okay, you write down anything you can. Do you need anything?"

Lana casually sipped her drink. "No, thank you."

Barry walked into the conference room where all hell was breaking loose. "Are you hearing all this shit?"

Peterson was all business. "How credible do you think she is?"

Barry scratched his head. "I don't know; she's pretty convincing. Maybe we should check out one of the schools."

"Okay, go back in and keep her talking. Get as much information as you can. We'll test out some of this information on Muhammad."

***

Agent Price brought a sandwich into Muhammad. "Hungry?"

"Yeah. Thanks. Can you take off these handcuffs?"

"Sure." He unlocked his hands and added a bottle of water. "What can you tell me about pipe bombs?"

Muhammad froze. His eyes narrowed, and his shoulders hunched over as he chewed his mouthful of sandwich.

"I want you to tell me everything you can. It's critical that you cooperate with us. The others have told their stories, and we want to see if you are going to tell the truth."

Muhammad fidgeted in his seat while sweat stained his shirt. He squinted at Agent Price and crossed his arms. "What did they say?"

"They told us about the pipe bombs and where they are."

Muhammad licked his lips and sputtered, "I-I didn't do anything with them. I-I just drove the car."

"Where are they?"

Muhammad's nostrils flared, and his breath became labored. "I don't know."

"Where did you drive the car?"

Muhammad stared down at his shaking hands. "This is a trick. Yousef would never tell you that."

"Do you really want all those innocent children to die?"

Muhammad's head snapped up, and his eyes flew wide. The truth was written all over his face. The bombs were at the schools.

Agent Price pushed the pad of paper across the table. "You know. It's not too late for you. Tell us where they are. I'll be back. You write down as much as you can remember."

Price walked back into the conference room behind the two-way mirror. "He just confirmed there are bombs, and that at least some are in schools. I think it's a credible threat."

The lead agent nodded. "I agree. We'll alert the bomb unit, and meanwhile let's collect as much intelligence as possible. Muhammad needs to believe the other two have both cooperated, especially Yousef."

Chapter 28
The Scramble

Monday, May 9th, 10:30 p.m.

Agent Peterson was barking orders.

"Evacuate all personnel immediately from the schools on the list, and any residences close to bomb sites.

"Get the DC Superintendent of Schools on the phone and tell him we have a credible threat and he needs to cancel all schools for tomorrow.

"Tell local law enforcement to set up perimeters around the schools. Call the command center and tell them to call the FBI bomb unit. Tell them we'll need robots, dogs, and bomb technicians."

Agent Barry stood with his arms crossed. "What about the girl?"

Peterson's brows were knitted into a single furry line across his forehead. "Bring her."

Floodlights lit up the playground of the first school on the list. A bomb-sniffing dog was let out of the SUV and ran straight to the bench.

Lana pointed at the brightly painted metal bench with wide tubular legs in the middle of the playground. "There is a bomb in the right front leg. Just loosen bolt on side and pull up the seat, you'll see it."

Bomber was the best bomb-sniffing dog in the K9 unit. He was barking at the bench when he was pulled away and loaded back into the SUV. The bomb technician approached the bench and disassembled the seat. He looked over his shoulder and nodded to confirm a visual, then carefully retrieved the pipe bomb and slowly placed it in a container.

The driver of the bomb unit's van, Anna, watched while the bomb technician, Chris, approached the van. She spoke into the radio clipped to her shoulder. "You need me to step out, Chris?"

"No, just sit tight."

Chris climbed into the back of a large, black van designed especially for the bomb squad. He loosened the end caps on the plastic pipe and spotted a timer. He delicately snipped the wires and disassembled the detonator from the timer. Only then did he heave a sigh of relief and remove his helmet.

He fished his phone out of his pocket and called Agent Peterson. "Good news is the intel is good. She led us straight to the source. Simple bomb encased in PVC with end caps. Bad news is, it had a timer set to go off in twelve hours."

Agent Peterson sucked in a breath, tightening the muscles in his jaw. He spoke in a steady, low-pitched voice. "You need to take the girl to each of the seven schools on the list and the Botanical Gardens."

Chris signaled Anna to go to the next school. The van pulled out behind a police unit clearing their way. "On it."

Agent Peterson spoke into the earpieces of the agents interrogating Yousef and Muhammad. "Get them talking about the bridges and tunnels. The schools are a verified threat."

He called the IT lab for more updates on Ahmed's laptop. "Have you noticed any names that could be bridges or tunnels?"

"Negative, but we've got a lead on the purchase of the bombs. A unit is approaching the residence as we speak. If we can find out the number of bombs purchased, we will know how many are left. A unit just finished searching Ahmed's residence in a motel in Anacostia. Turned up a few clothes and toiletries, but that's it."

Peterson checked the time, 12:05 a.m. "Okay. Let me know."

Agent Meng was coordinating the search. When they arrived at the second school, he took a simpler approach. "Okay, gather round. Let's have the local police set up a perimeter around the playground. Let's kill the floodlights and drive the van up to the bench. We'll use the van's headlights for illumination, and it's less distance to carry the bomb."

Meng crossed his arms and glared at Lana. "Where's this one?"

Lana pointed across the playground to the bench next to the monkey bars. "It's in the right front leg."

"Is that where all of them are going to be?"

"Yes."

"Okay, let's confirm the intel with Bomber." The dog sniffed his way around the playground until he stopped and sat in front of the bench. "Call him back and move to the next site. Once we've cleared here, everyone get to the next school ASAP. Same protocol. Police get the playground fence open and surround the perimeter. We'll be there shortly."

Once again, Agent Chris Ruby approached the bench in full bomb gear. He loosened the bolts and found the same type of pipe bomb. He nodded and flashed a thumbs-up before fishing the bomb out of the bench. He placed it in the container carefully, and walked softly back to the van.

Anna called back after she saw him separate the materials into the different secure containers, "You ready to move?"

Chris nodded. "Let's go."

The rest of the night and into the early morning followed the same procedures with less and less fanfare. Lana's information was spot on until they wove through rush hour traffic to the Botanical Gardens.

A chain link fence surrounded all the schools. In most cases the night custodian or principal was waiting for them and opened the delivery gate when they arrived. But when they approached the Botanical Gardens, the tall iron gates surrounding the garden area were closed and locked.

It took a while before they were able to locate security and open the gates. Once inside the garden, they found out the bench had moved due to recent construction.

Lana was adamantly pointing at the trellised area next to the stage. "The bench was under the arbor. It's gone."

Meng let out a heavy sigh. "Send out Bomber."

The garden area was very different from the open playground. Trees, bushes, flowers and water gardens were everywhere. The maze of paths wove around the foliage.

Bomber sniffed around the trees and down the different paths. He stopped under the trellis but didn't bark. He followed along the fence and then doubled back.

Everyone was getting nervous. They were next to the heart of DC. The traffic along Independence Ave was honking, and had turned into a parking lot, everyone gawking at the police cars surrounding the perimeter of the Botanical Gardens.

Someone called out, "Traffic is gridlocked all around DC because of our search. We need to get traffic cops out here quick."

Meng checked his watch. 7:35 a.m. He could hardly hear himself think over all the traffic and chaos, which, even worse, still was building. "Let's move the perimeter. The bench isn't inside the fence. Let's get these streets closed off."

The police redirected traffic and set barriers until the streets around the Botanical Gardens were finally empty.

Bomber returned to Chris's side and sat, signaling he didn't find anything. Chris patted the dog. "Good boy."

Meng's voice called out through Chris's earpiece. "What do you think?"

Chris answered, "I don't think it's here. Call the person in charge of construction. Ask him where the bench went."

Meng stood back on the sidewalk with his arms crossed, his stance combative. "Copy that." He glanced to the left at the American Indian Museum, and farther down at the Air and Space Museum. He turned to the right and stared at the Capitol.

"Chris?"

"Yeah, Ray."

"What kind of power does the bomb have?"

"It was designed to kill and wound people, not to blow up buildings."

Meng checked his watch again. 8:05. "Okay. Let's stand down. Everybody back to their cars and off the streets. Let's get the traffic moving."

Chris walked back to the SUV with Bomber and gave him a treat before heading back to the van. He climbed up into the passenger seat and joined Anna in the cab.

Anna handed him a bottle of water. "So what are we doing now?"

Chris pulled off his headgear and gulped the bottle of water. "Thanks. I was told to sit tight while they find out who moved the bench.

By 9:00, news teams were lining the perimeter, against the advice of the police. Ray stood with his back to them, ignoring their requests. He had talked to the head of security inside the Botanical Gardens and got the name of the construction company responsible for the removal of the bench. He left a message on the number he was given, but still hadn't received a call back.

Chapter 29
Bill's TSL

Monday, May 9th, 9:00 p.m.

Emma was escorted up the elevator, where an agent was sitting in a wide marbled foyer.

Agent Coffman stood to greet her. "Emma Carr?"

Emma nodded, "Yes."

The elevator closed behind her as the other agent left, and Agent Coffman opened the apartment door. "You should have everything you need."

She walked Emma into the kitchen. "The kitchen is stocked with dinner, breakfast, and snacks. If you need anything else, I can send for it."

Emma nodded, looking around the well-equipped kitchen. She followed the agent through the plush living room and down the short hall to two bedrooms.

The agent escorted her into the smaller of the two. "This one is yours. You should find some clothes in the closet, along with a robe and toiletries in the bathroom."

"Okay. Thanks."

"If you want to use the TV, there are instructions for the controls and games in the drawer of the coffee table."

"Okay."

Emma perused the refrigerator then found an individual-sized Ben and Jerry's ice cream in the freezer. She grabbed a spoon and settled in front of the T.V.

An hour and a half later, Karen walked in the door.

"Mom!"

Karen ran to Emma on the couch and held her. "Are you okay? Oh, my God. I heard about Blake. Oh honey, I'm so sorry."

Emma sobbed into Karen's arms. After a bit, her sobs reduced to sniffles. "Did they catch who did it?"

"I think so. We'll know more when your dad gets here, which should be any minute now."

Emma tucked her hair behind her ears and grabbed a nearby tissue to wipe her nose. "I can't believe I'm never going to see him again. If I'd known that was the last time I'd ever see him, I would have hugged him longer." Her voice broke. "I would tell him to stay at the bar. I want to tell him…" Emma choked on a sob and wiped at the tears. "I would tell him how sorry I am, and that I loved him."

Karen held her while she wept. "He knows. He will always know, 'cause he'll always be in your heart."

When they were all cried out, they put the frozen pizza in the oven. Karen caught a glimpse of herself in the ornate mirror. "I'm a mess. I've got to get out of these clothes and take a shower."

Twenty minutes later, Karen walked out in a robe, combing through her wet hair. "Did your dad get here yet?"

Emma shook her head and took the last bite of her pizza. "Not yet. I can barely keep my eyes open; I keep nodding off. I need to go to bed."

Karen put a slice on a plate and glanced at the clock on the wall, 11:25. "You go on. I'm going to be right behind you."

Bill finished his briefing on the pipe bomb situation and left to join Karen and Emma at the apartment. By the time he arrived, the apartment was quiet. He peeked in at each of them sleeping and walked back to the kitchen and stared into the refrigerator. He put a slice of cold pizza on a plate and poured a stiff drink from the bar. The last two day's events weighed heavy on his eyelids. After downing the last of his drink, he took a quick shower and slipped into bed next to Karen. Their bed was always his safe haven, an island away from the world's problems.

Karen mumbled sleepily, "Is it over?"

Bill slipped his arm around her waist and pulled her close. "It never is. Go back to sleep. We're fine." He kissed the top of her head and smelled the familiar girl from his youth.

Chapter 30
Morning Meeting

Tuesday, May 10th, 9:00 a.m.

Jessica spotted Bill through the glass wall in her office when he walked toward his. She frantically waved him into her office. "Did you hear they couldn't find the last bomb?"

Bill shook his head. "No, I just got here. What's going on?"

"It was supposed to be at the Botanical Gardens, but the bench it was planted in is gone. All intel has been good up until now. They are on standby until they can reach the construction crew who moved the bench."

"Who is in charge of the search?"

"Ray Meng."

Bill ran his hand over his face and checked his watch. 9:05 a.m. "He's good. They'll find it. If it's set to detonate at noon, they have less than three hours."

Jessica winced when she tried to stand.

"Hey, how are you doing?"

"I'm good, just sore from being thrown around yesterday. Listen, I've got some thoughts I want to run by you when you have the time."

"Regarding?"

"The leak. I think I know how that cover page was compromised."

Bill took a seat in the chair across from Jessica's desk. "Let's hear it."

Jessica leaned back in her chair. "When I pulled that veil off Lana's face and saw her platinum blonde hair, I was shocked. She looked so familiar to me. Last night, in the apartment, I was eating a Reuben sandwich, and it reminded me of seeing Jared, the IT guy, in the cafeteria. He was showing a picture on his phone to everyone, claiming it was his girlfriend. I only caught a glimpse of the picture, but it looked a lot like Lana."

Bill pinched his eyebrows and crossed his legs. "That's a little out there."

Jessica leaned forward, putting her elbows on her desk. "Stay with me. I was looking over the notes from last night's interrogations they faxed over. Listen to this, the agent asked her where she got the list with the names and she answers:

I saw a guy on Facebook who worked for the FBI. I friended him and talked to him. Sent him my picture. He thinks I am his girlfriend. I asked him to prove to me he work for FBI. One day we meet and walk around DC. He showed me his phone of a list he said was top secret. He said he worked on important cases. He left his phone on the table, and I took a picture of his list on my phone and gave it to Ahmed. Ahmed matched the names on list to names and addresses from the government files that were hacked, and matched names to addresses near here, then we pledged their deaths to ISIL.

Jessica arched her left brow. "So the question is…how does she know the guy on Facebook works for the FBI *before* she friends him?"

Bill shrugged and looked expectantly at Jessica.

Jessica continued, "Well, my guess is he snapped a selfie in front of the FBI logo downstairs and used it as his profile pic.

"Remember when you accused me of having something to do with your computer freezing?"

Bill crossed his arms. "Yeah."

"Well, Jared asked if he could take control of your computer, didn't he?"

"Yeah."

"What if he posted a selfie in front of the FBI logo *inside* the building on his Facebook profile. Anyone familiar with the FBI knows you are not allowed to bring cell phones into the building. She pegs him for an easy target right off the bat. She friends him and sends him her picture. They meet, he tries to impress her by showing her a top-secret cover sheet of an ongoing operation, and she takes a picture of the cover sheet."

Bill remained quiet.

"I checked the IT records. He took control of your screen on May 7th. I also checked the login file of the Syrian Op. You logged in that day."

Bill's eyes widened with acknowledgement.

"What if he took a screen shot of the cover page of Syrian Op #702 from your frozen computer?"

Bill rubbed his hand down his face. "May 8, we received the threat that included the names of all those involved in the Syrian Op."

Jessica leaned back in her chair. "Yep."

Bill reached back and shut the door. "All this started because he was trying to impress a girl?" A wave of red started at his neck and washed over his face. Even his ears were burning red. "An entire family was murdered. We have spent hundreds of man hours and tens of thousands of dollars in resources chasing down a leak because some kid got a *hard on!?* That is just *great*. He shook his head with disgust. This is going to be a black eye for the FBI."

Jessica bit her lower lip and nodded. "Does it have to become public? We stopped a major terrorist attack and exposed a sleeper cell. We should be able to take a victory lap for that."

Bill leaned forward, resting his forearms on his thighs. "If he hadn't posted his pic or shown her that sheet, we wouldn't have known about this sleeper cell or stopped those attacks. They would still be out there, and I hate to think about what today would have looked like."

Silence sat between them.

Jessica tore at the edges of a paper note. "We worked the intelligence and busted a sleeper cell. We *did* stop those attacks."

"Yeah, but if this gets out, the media will spin it much differently. They will play this like another Edward Snowden. We hired a young contractor and gave him security clearances, and he burned us. Same story—different agency.

Jessica rolled her eyes. "This is hardly the same." She tried to bring levity to the conversation. "This story has a much happier ending."

Bill shrugged his shoulders. "Still treason. He could go to prison. It's a shame; we could use him."

Jessica leaned back in her chair. "Okay, let's say we *can* keep it quiet. What if we put him in a minimum-security prison or house arrest and made him a plant on social media? Who's to say this won't work again? We can say this was our plan all along. We use Jared to troll for sleeper cells by posting his FBI mug for bait. He works the contacts. We look like geniuses."

Bill stood and put his hand on the door handle. "It could work. But we need to prove this first. I've got a one o'clock briefing with the Deputy Director and the Interrogation Unit. Let's meet after that and put together a plan."

Jessica smiled. "Yes, sir. I'll make sure he is here in the building today. Should I set up a polygraph?"

"Excellent idea. Set up a meeting in my office for 2:30, and schedule the polygraph for 2:45."

"I'm on it."

Chapter 31
Park and Ride

Tuesday, May 10, 10:00.

Agent Meng held up his finger to pause the conversation he was having with the officer. He grabbed his phone. "Meng."

"Yeah, this is Manuel Reyes. I was given this number and told there was some kind of emergency."

Meng stuck his finger in his other ear to block the noise. "We are trying to locate a bench you moved from the Botanical Gardens."

"I was told I could have it. They were throwing it out."

"Where is it now?"

"I gave it to one of the guys who works for me."

"What is his address?"

"I don't know, man."

Meng pinched his eyes shut and counted to three to keep from losing his temper. "There may be a bomb in the leg of that bench. We need to find it."

"Jeez, man! Why didn't you say that to begin with? It's in the back of his truck at one of my work sites. Hang on, while I find out where he is."

Meng heard a string of Spanish that sounded like curse words.

Reyes came back on the phone. "He's on the second floor of Union Station."

"Can you call him?"

"Look man, he's illegal. Okay? He doesn't have a phone or speak English."

"What about a supervisor or someone with him?"

"Let me check. I'll call you back."

Five minutes later, Meng's phone rang. "Meng."

"They said the guy just left on break. It'll be another fifteen minutes. I'm headed over there. It'll take me a while to wade through traffic. Something's got the area around the Capitol in gridlock."

"Okay. Keep trying, and call me back if you reach him."

Meng called Chris on the radio. "Chris?"

"Yeah, Ray. What'd ya find out?"

"It's in the back of a truck, possibly parked at Union Station."

"Are you kidding me?"

"Nope. I'm going to get the Capitol Police to clear a path through traffic for you. Can you put Bomber and his handler in your van so we don't have to try and get all these vehicles over there?"

"No problem. Where's the truck?"

"I'm guessing in the garage or somewhere close. I really have no idea. There's no way to clear those garages of cars, but we can evacuate the people. What kind of damage are we talking about?"

"Just depends where it is. Like I said, it won't blow up a building, but it'll kill or injure everyone within a forty-yard radius."

"Get Bomber and be ready. I'll get your lead car."

Agent Meng made a number of phone calls, and within minutes, police sirens were escorting the van with Chris, Anna, Bomber and his handler to Union Station.

Meng parked behind the van and the police escort. "I'm going to go in and try and find the guy. Sit tight."

Meng was headed up the escalator when his phone rang. "Meng."

"This is Reyes. Got a hold of my guy. He didn't drive into today. He says the truck is parked at a Park and Ride off Route 50 by Davidsonville."

"Is the bench in the back?"

"As far as I know."

"ASK HIM!" Meng was ready to lose it by the time he hung up. He waited for another three minutes, 10: 45. He was racing around the second floor, looking for a construction crew when his phone rang again. "Meng."

"Bench is in the back of his truck."

"Thanks." Meng disconnected and called Chris. "Tell the police we need an escort to the Park and Ride off 50 in Davidsonville. The truck is there."

"Is there anyone at the Annapolis RA (Resident Agency)? It might be quicker. We are cutting this pretty close with traffic."

Meng scratched his head and ran his hand down the back of his neck. "Head out. I'll see if I can get someone closer, but let's not count on it."

"On it."

Agent Meng called the Annapolis police. They sent their emergency response team to the parking lot and evacuated all persons. They taped off a forty-yard perimeter around the area and rerouted Rt. 424, causing Interstate 50 and 301 to back up, making the DC bomb unit crawl down Interstate 50.

Meng wove through traffic in his SUV, using the emergency lane and the grassy median.

Chris called the Annapolis ERT, Emergency Response Team, to share the possible location of the bomb and proper procedures to follow.

"This is Chris Ruby. I'm an FBI bomb specialist. Who am I talking to?"

"My name is Nathan Beers. I'm with the Annapolis Emergency Response Team." Nathan was the youngest member of the team. He had completed his training less than a month earlier, and had been on the job for less than a year. He took the lead to deactivate the bomb to prove his worth to his fellow officers and impress the FBI.

"Okay, Nathan. Loosen the side bolt of the seat and look into the right front tubular leg of the bench." He waited for a response.

He was on speakerphone with Chris. "I've detached the seat, and I'm looking down the right front leg, but there is nothing there."

"Check the other legs."

"The bottom of the legs are open. I can see up into the tubular legs. They look like they were sawed off from a concrete base. There is nothing there. What is it I'm supposed to be looking for?"

Chris closed his eyes and shook his head at the idea the young bomb tech would take the time to unbolt the seat when the legs were already cut open. "You are looking for a white PCV pipe with caps on each end. It's about a foot long, two inches in diameter."

Nathan looked around the contents in the truck and spotted the pipe bomb rolling free in the bed of the truck. "I think I've found it." Nervous sweat ran down his back as he picked up the plastic pipe. "One end cap is cracked."

Chris could hear the nerves in Nathan's voice. He checked the clock on the dash. 11:30. "We've got less than thirty minutes to disable the bomb. I'm just passing route 3, and the traffic is almost a parking lot. Do you want me to walk you through it?"

Nathan was riding on false bravado when he said, "If it didn't detonate rolling around in the back of this truck, I should be okay. Go ahead." Although, even as he said the words, he could feel his guts turning to liquid.

"Okay. Feel for the lightest end of the pipe and pull off the cap on the lightest end. You will see a small, round, digital timer attached to a yellow and red wire. Snip the RED wire. Do you copy that?"

"Copy that."

Meng pulled up outside the yellow tape and watched from his car. He radioed to Chris. "You talking to this guy with the bomb?"

Chris put his phone on mute and answered Ray on the radio. "Yeah. How's he look?"

"Young."

All communications were silent.

The heavy bomb gear seemed to get heavier and hotter as Nathan twisted the end cap off. "The cap is off."

"Okay. Do you see the red and yellow wires?"

"Yeah."

"Gently clip the red wire."

Panic rose in Nathan's voice. "I see the digital timer, but it's not going. It says zero." He tried to swallow the lump in his throat, but his throat was too dry.

Chris was having an *oh shit* moment. "Clip the red wire, Nathan."

Nathan held his breath and gently manipulated the red wire, snipping it away from the timer. He closed his eyes in anticipation of a possible detonation…and then it was…over. He gave a thumbs-up, and everyone around him applauded. He blurted out to Chris on the speakerphone. "Device is disabled." Then turned, ripped his head gear off and immediately vomited in the grass.

Chris heard him retching, closed his eyes and started breathing again. "Nicely done," he said when Nathan came back on the line. "I can see the exit and will be there in less than five minutes."

Meng greeted the bomb unit when they pulled into the lot. "A little too close for comfort."

Chris climbed down from the cab with a container. "Tell me about it." He joined Nathan at the truck and congratulated him, then separated the bomb pieces into the different containers and headed back to DC.

Meng called Peterson once he was on the road. "We've got the all-clear on the ones we know about. Did IT come up with more intel from the computer?"

"No they didn't. But nice job, Ray. Go home and get some sleep. I'll catch up with you later."

"Roger that." Ray hung up and headed home.

Chapter 32
Moving Forward

Tuesday, May 10, 10:30 a.m.

Karen did a last check around the apartment and joined Emma in the kitchen. "You ready to go home?"

"My car is at my apartment, so I need to go back there first. The sublets are moving in day after tomorrow."

Karen frowned at Emma. "I don't want you to go back there by yourself. I'll tell you what, let's get a ride back to the marina so I can get my car, and I'll take you back to your apartment. That way we'll have two cars to load your stuff into."

"Thanks, Mom. I also want to see if my phone is still at the marina. I can imagine the messages I've missed."

Karen stood and threw her BOB bag over her shoulder. "You ready?"

Emma almost regretted leaving the safe cocoon of the apartment where she had been cut off from outside communications. For the first time she could remember, she dreaded checking her phone and computer. She inhaled a deep breath and mentally put on emotional armor so she could tackle the next few hours. "Yeah, Mom. Let's go."

Agent Coffman was back on duty outside the apartment door. She smiled when Karen and Emma emerged from the apartment. "Good morning. If you're ready, I'm your driver."

Karen raised her brows at Emma, questioning if she was ready, and Emma nodded. "Thanks. My car is parked at the marina in Annapolis, and then we are going to go to Georgetown and move Emma's things out of her apartment. Do you think that will be a problem?"

"I'll escort you back to Georgetown from the marina so you'll have access to the crime scene."

Emma winced when her house was referred to as a crime scene. She kept imagining Blake's lifeless body in the alley, and could feel her breathing hitch as sobs threatened to erupt again. Tears burned her eyes when she thought about the call she still needed to make to his parents.

Her life felt like an endless nightmare. Her mom squeezed her hand. Emma steeled her self-control and replied, "Thank you. That will be helpful."

As soon as they pulled out of the parking garage, they were stuck in traffic. All streets were gridlocked. Agent Coffman turned on the radio for the traffic report. The announcer was reporting detours and traffic problems around DC. "Something must be going on; they've shut down all the streets around the Botanical Gardens and the Capitol. It's going to be a while before we get out of DC."

An hour and forty-five minutes later, they reached the marina. Karen pulled her purse from her BOB bag and fished out her keys.

Emma walked away from the parking lot toward the restaurant. "Wait here, Mom, okay? I'm going to see if anyone turned in my phone. I left it in the bathroom."

Five minutes later, Emma walked out of the restaurant, blinking and wiping her eyes, her attention glued to her phone while she scrolled through message after message from friends expressing their condolences. She climbed into the passenger side of Karen's car and showed her mother the phone. "Look at all these messages."

"You have a lot of friends, and a lot of support, honey. You are going to get through this."

On the ride into Georgetown, Emma checked her Facebook page. Hundreds of friends had posted pictures of her and Blake at different college events and expressed their love and support. She put her phone down to dry her eyes with a tissue and blow her nose.

She typed in a post. "Thanks to everyone for the kind words. This is a nightmare. Your love and friendship mean a lot to me."

Within seconds, she received reply after reply asking where she was and how she was doing. Emma couldn't begin to answer each and every reply. She typed a vague post. "Coping with the news. Will be in touch."

She switched over to Blake's Facebook page, and was heartbroken all over again while she read the outpouring of love from his friends and family, posting their love and last memories of him. She put the phone on her lap, grabbed more tissues and sobbed.

Karen and Emma parked behind Agent Coffman in front of Emma's apartment while the agent ducked under the yellow tape and approached the officer guarding the crime scene. She got permission to remove Emma's belongings and waved from the front porch for them to join her.

Karen rested her hand on Emma's shoulder. "Are you ready to do this?"

Emma wiped her eyes one last time and took a deep breath. She put her hand on the door handle and nodded. "I have to call Blake's parents when we get home."

"I thought you did that yesterday?"

Emma's red eyes were downcast. "I chickened out."

Emma looked around at the fingerprinting dust covering the walls, doors, and counters. Blood splatters on the kitchen floor were marked with numbers. "I need to call the sublet. There's no way they'll be able to live here over the summer. I'm sorry, Mom. It's going to cost another $4,500 for the next three months if I don't sublet it."

"We'll do something. It won't take three months. Let's not worry about money and the sublet right now."

"Mom, she's supposed to move in here in two days."

"One problem at a time. Let's get this stuff moved."

Emma wondered if the girl who was supposed to sublet would even want to move in after she heard someone had been murdered there. She stepped over the little numbered evidence markers around the apartment and loaded her belongings into their cars.

Two hours later, they said goodbye to Agent Coffman and drove back to Annapolis. Karen hit the garage door button above the windshield of her car and glanced over at Peggy's house. The house was dark and curtains were drawn.

Karen and Emma pulled in to the garage next to each other. "Let's stack the boxes you aren't going to use right away against the wall and carry your clothes in first."

Emma's eyes grew big as she stared over Karen's shoulder. "Mom, the door is open."

Karen froze then slowly turned around. "I probably left it open. I was in a hurry when I left here." She picked up the baseball bat leaning against the shelf and walked toward the door.

"Mom, don't go in there."

"Emma, stay here."

"MOM! DON'T!" Emma shrieked. "Look what happened to Blake."

"Emma, it's all right. Those men are in custody. We wouldn't have been allowed to come home if it wasn't safe."

Karen nudged the door open with the bat, then stepped inside. She glanced around the family room, finding everything just as she left it. The coffee pot was full of cold coffee, and her phone was right where she left it on the counter. She stood in the middle of the kitchen, searching for signs of something out of place. Everything was peaceful. It was a relief to be back with the comforts of home.

She walked back out to the garage and picked up an armful of clothes on hangers. "I told you. It's nothing. I'm sure I just left the door open."

Emma followed Karen upstairs to her bedroom and noted she still had the bat.

Karen stopped abruptly at the top of the stairs when she heard noises coming from Emma's room.

Chapter 33
Debriefing

Tuesday, May 10, 1:00 p.m.

Bill poured a cup of coffee and took a seat at the conference table.

As soon as the Deputy Director walked in, the meeting began.

The first person scheduled to speak was Special Agent in Charge Peterson.

Peterson remained seated, addressing the table through red eyes and a hoarse voice. He rubbed his hand over his morning stubble and set aside his coffee. "At approximately 10:30 last night, we followed through on intelligence received from one of the ISIL cell members Agent Murphy apprehended yesterday. The subject confirmed the information we pulled from the recovered laptop. She led us to seven pipe bombs planted at elementary schools in DC. Our bomb units were able to disable all of them, with the exception of one that had been moved. The Annapolis ERT coordinated efforts with our guys and was able to disable that one.

"A SWAT team acted on intel found on the laptop taken from Ahmed, the deceased cell member. They located the residence of the person who made and sold the bombs. When they raided the home, they found a young family in the upstairs of the home and a bomb-making factory in the walkout basement they rented out to another person on a cash basis.

"The bombs were all set to detonate at noon today. They were planted in the middle of school playgrounds so they would do maximum damage at noon recess.

"Here is a sketch of the man who rents the basement space. We are still investigating threats to bridges and tunnels, but we are hoping that, since they didn't detonate at noon, they don't exist. Questions?"

Bill spoke up. "Where are the *alleged* terrorists now?"

"They are still at the barn. The two who are cooperative, Muhammad and Lana, are in dorm rooms, but Yousef is in lockup."

***

Lana lay back against the pillow with her hands tucked behind her head. She was watching the constant loop of Christian programming on the overhead TV that she assumed was propaganda. She wondered if the others had given up the rest of their plan since Ahmed was dead. There was no mention of it from the agents. She answered all their questions truthfully—they just hadn't asked her the right questions.

What would the other cells think when they didn't hear anything from Ahmed? Their attacks were the signal to ignite a chain reaction, knocking down the first of a set of dominos waiting in place around the country. Would they continue with the attacks if they didn't see the targeted schools and buildings in DC destroyed?

***

Next on the agenda was Assistant Director Bill Carr.

Bill cleared his throat. "Agent Murphy was responsible for apprehending Lana, the female. Ahmed and Lana grabbed and drugged her yesterday, and held her in a basement. She escaped. Ahmed was shot and killed. He is believed to be the organizer of the group. His computer proved to have valuable intelligence for both here and in Syria.

"We are monitoring his contacts in Syria. The operation was not blown. There have been no changes to our surveillance, with the exception of the two personnel who have been pulled. We are putting Campbell back in the field, while Jennings is being flown back today, and we have assigned personnel to him to help with funeral arrangements and counseling.

"We have reached out to our contacts with the Mexican Cartel on the border. They assure us they want no part of ISIL using their tunnels as passages. They appear to be cooperating with us, and we have threatened extra pressure on them if they associate with persons known to have ties to ISIL.

"We retrieved several lists of *friends* who have helped the sleeper cell. These are Americans who are ISIL sympathizers. We are running background checks on all the names today. We have created a list of persons of interest and will be strictly monitoring their activities. Questions?"

Peterson glared at those around the table, practically daring them to ask another question that would prolong the meeting. He had been up all night and wanted to go home and sleep.

The Deputy Director nodded approval. "Do we know how this cell got the list of names in the first place?"

"Not yet sir, but Agent Murphy and I have a working theory that we hope to prove later this afternoon."

The room dispersed, and Bill went to find Jessica. When he reached his office, his secretary gave him a worried expression.

"Sir, your daughter called and asked that you call home."

"Did she say what it was about?"

"No, but she sounded upset."

Bill read the message and walked into his office. He took a seat at his desk and dialed home.

Emma answered on the first ring. "Dad?"

He could hear the panic in her voice. "What's the matter?"

"Peggy broke into our house and is going crazy on Mom and me. She trashed my room and is out of her mind. Should I call the police?"

Bill dropped his forehead into his hand. He could imagine Peggy's grief and anger. They'd been neighbors and friends for so long, although he had always considered her a little unstable where her boys were concerned. Up until now, he thought she was just an overprotective mom. "Does she have a weapon?"

"She's got my golf club, and Mom has my ball bat."

Bill could hear the two women hurling insults while objects hit the floor in the background and imagined a scene out of vaudeville. "Emma, let me talk to your mom."

Emma handed the phone to Karen.

Karen reluctantly accepted the phone. "Bill?"

"What's going on? How did she get in?"

"She's had our key for ten years!"

Emma pleaded in the background. "Peggy, put down that lamp. I had nothing to do with this."

Peggy screamed back, smashing the lamp. "*Liar!* Cal would never be in this trouble if it weren't for *you!*"

Karen tucked the phone between her ear and shoulder. She swung the bat at Peggy and let out a string of obscenities.

Bill listened to the F bombs detonating on the other end of the line. "Karen, calm down."

Karen stiffened and sounded out each syllable, "Don't. Tell. Me. To calm down," then she dropped the phone to the carpet.

Bill closed his eyes and shook his head. *When would he ever learn?*

Emma picked up the phone. "Dad, what should I do?"

Bill was mentally darting through alternatives. He tried to see the one that would de-escalate the situation the fastest. "You and your mom need to leave. Go sit in the car or go next door and see if any of Peggy's family is home. I'll send someone, but not the police. Not yet."

Emma shouted at her mom in the hallway. "Mom, let's go. Dad said for us to get out of here."

"Emma, you go to the car. I'll be right there."

"Mom…"

"Go."

Emma knew that look of unrelenting stubbornness. She walked out of the room and sat on the stairs to listen.

Karen lowered the ball bat slowly. "Peggy, this is insane. Do you realize Emma's boyfriend is dead? Those horrible kids killed him—slit his throat. It could have been Emma. Who is to say Cal wasn't going to be next?"

Peggy was crying and shouting, "He didn't do this!"

Karen dropped her bat and approached Peggy slowly. "I never said he did, Peggy. He's a victim, too. We all are."

Peggy lowered the golf club and sank down onto the bed. "Our names are all over the news. They are calling my son a terrorist. They all think we are part of ISIL. You have no idea what we have been through in the last twenty-four hours."

Karen closed her eyes and sighed. Tears rolled down her cheeks. "My last twenty-four hours haven't been a picnic, either. I'm very sorry about Cal. I'm sorry your name is being dragged through the mud. But, Peggy, they have been chasing us all over creation trying to kill us for the past twenty-four hours. These people are pure evil."

Peggy stood and stared out the window. "Why? How did all this happen?"

Karen sat on the bed and shook her head. "I don't know."

Peggy bit her lip and looked at Karen. "Did you know that *girl* has been emailing with Cal for over a year? She tricked him into this. Cal is devastated. He claims he is in love with her."

Karen knelt down and started picking up pieces of broken lamp and knickknacks. "Well, both our kids are devastated, then. Poor Blake—and his parents…at least we aren't planning our children's funerals today."

Peggy squatted down and helped pick up the mess she had created. "I'm sorry, Karen. I was listening to the news, and they said Emma had identified Cal as one of the possible terrorists. I just lost it."

"That is either poor journalism or good sensationalism. You can't listen to them. The media uses this stuff for ratings."

"But everybody believes it! Our lives are ruined."

"None of our lives will ever be the same. We have to be grateful for what we still have and move forward."

Emma saw a car pull up and went outside to meet them.

Agent Marcs pulled into the driveway and greeted Emma, showing his badge and introducing himself. "Everything okay? Your dad…er… I mean the Assistant Director asked me to come here and remove someone from the property."

"I think it's over. I can't hear what they are saying, but they aren't trying to kill each other anymore."

"You want to call your father and tell him? See what he wants me to do?"

Chapter 34
You're Fired

Tuesday, May 10th, 2:30 p.m.

Jessica knocked on Bill's door at exactly 2:30. "You ready for me?"

Bill waved her in. "Yeah, come in and sit down."

Jessica sat across from Bill's desk and crossed her legs. "Jared is meeting us in the conference room down the hall. The polygraph is all set up there, so when he walks in, it should scare the crap out of him first thing."

"Good." Bill handed her a sealed envelope.

"What's this?"

"Expediency."

Jessica opened the envelope and read the letter issuing her a three-day unpaid suspension for breaking protocol and calling Liam. "This says it starts Friday the 13th? No review board?"

"The Deputy Director thought this would be in everyone's best interest. This gives us the rest of the week to tie up loose ends, you are punished, and you get a five-day weekend. Since Liam is recovering for the next week or so, I thought this might help everyone."

Jessica tucked the letter back in the envelope. She knew others had received far worse punishments for similar infractions. "Thank you."

Bill ran his hand down his tie and chose his words carefully. "The Deputy Director doesn't feel the same benevolence toward Jared. He wants him fired *immediately* if this is true. He is to be escorted from our meeting out the front door. He will also be charged. He wants to send a clear message to everyone that we have zero tolerance for leaks of any kind. He especially wants to drive home the fact that Jared's actions resulted in the deaths of an innocent family."

Jessica's shoulders sagged. "Did you tell him our plan?"

Bill nodded. "I did. He said we could use anyone's picture to accomplish the same thing. We have departments set up to monitor social media and pursue perceived threats. He was adamant. Jared is out. He proved he is not to be trusted."

Jessica nodded and let out a sigh. "That's true."

Bill checked the time. "It's 2:35, let's do this."

***

Jared's knees were bouncing nervously, and his resting heart rate was 120 when he checked his fitness band. The polygraph equipment at the end of the long, polished table sat like an accuser staring at him. His mind was racing through different possibilities for why he had been summoned when Bill and Jessica walked into the room.

They greeted him and took the seats across from him. Jessica noticed the pit stains on his shirt and sat quietly next to Bill.

Bill led the interview. "Jared, do you know why you are here?"

Jared shook his head. "No, sir."

He placed Lana's photo on the table in front of Jared. "Do you know this girl?"

Jared's eyes were wild. He kept wiping his sweaty palms on his thighs. "Yes."

"How did you meet her?"

"Uh…I…met her on Facebook."

"How long have you known her?"

Jared shrugged. "Maybe a couple of weeks."

"Do you know she is a terrorist?"

Jared bit his thumbnail and shook his head.

"Two military families were targeted yesterday, and one entire family was murdered because of the names she got off a cover sheet of a classified document. She's part of a sleeper cell that tried to blow up schools. All this from a leaked document."

Jared was sweating profusely.

"Did you take a screenshot of my computer screen?"

Jared glanced down at the polygraph equipment and wiped the sweat dripping into his eyes. He nodded and looked down at his folded hands on the table.

"Did you share that picture with this woman?"

Jared nodded. "Yes, sir. I'm sorry. I had no idea."

"You knew it was a classified document. You knew you were not to have a cell phone in this building. You knew you were never to take a picture of something from my computer."

"Yes, sir."

"I'll need your badges." Bill stared straight at Jared. "You are fired, and charges will be filed against you." He shoved a piece of paper in front of him. "This is a gag order. You are not to discuss what you did with anyone. If you obey this injunction, it will assure you get the lesser of the charges. If you should discuss with anyone that you copied a classified document and shared it with a terrorist, your charges will be treason, and we will push for the severest penalties. Do you understand?"

Jared nodded.

"I suggest you go home and get a lawyer. You are finished at the FBI." Bill stood and nodded to Jessica.

"Agent Murphy, would you escort him to security?"

Jessica stood. "Yes, sir."

Bill strode out of the room without looking back.

Jessica walked Jared to the elevator. When they stepped in, Jared pushed the button to his floor.

She shook her head. "Sorry, you are being escorted out the door. Your belongings will be delivered to you in the garage shortly. You can wait next to the guard shack."

They rode the rest of the way to the garage in complete silence. Jared's belongings were waiting for him when he stepped off the elevator. The security guard stepped forward, handed him a box, and escorted him to his car.

Chapter 35
A Kiss to Make it Better

Wednesday, May 11th, 7 p.m.

Jessica used her key to let herself into Liam's apartment. Jeb rushed past her and made a beeline to the back of the apartment. "Hey, anyone home?"

She set her purse next to the mail on the counter and looked around the sparse kitchen at the dirty dishes in the sink. She walked through the living room, where clothes were piled along the back of the L-shaped brown leather pit group. The curtains were pulled, and a laundry basket with clothes to fold was sitting on the floor. The only light was coming from the bathroom. She looked in and saw a wet towel on the floor and residue of shaving cream and toothpaste in the sink.

"Back here," called Liam.

Jessica walked down the hall to his bedroom and found Jeb stretched out next to Liam, who was propped up on the bed with pillows and a beer in his hand, watching a game on the TV. Jeb was resting his head on Liam's lap, while gazing up at him with his soulful brown eyes, and seeming to ask why Liam's arm was in a sling and his foot was taped and elevated.

She spotted the cooler next to the bed and opened the lid to find it full of beer and ice. "Cooler in the bedroom, *classy.*"

Liam pointed at his swollen ankle. "Easier to get to."

Jessica sat next to him on the bed. "Do you have everything you need?"

Liam wrapped his arm around her. "Cold beer and a warm woman in my bed, what more can a man want when he has a week off?"

"How about a warm beach?"

"Why the hell would I want a beach when I have a bed?"

Liam set his beer on the TV tray he used as a nightstand and gave Jessica a penetrating stare. "I understand you got three days off for calling me." He tugged her jacket off her shoulder.

Jessica shrugged out of her jacket and kicked off her shoes. "I did."

"What are you going to do with your time off?"

"I don't know. You got any ideas?"

Liam nudged Jeb to move over and pulled her under his covers. "I have a few."

She cuddled up next to him, trying to avoid his injuries, and laid her head on his chest.

A quiet calm settled around them.

Jeb stretched his legs and adjusted to the sleeping arrangement while still managing to take up half the bed. Liam took a pull from his beer and checked the score. He set his beer on the bedside table and ran his fingers through Jessica's hair. "You're quiet."

"Just thinkin'."

"What about?"

"Mostly about Lana. A while ago, I was asked to speak at a high school career day in the fall. I think I'm going to talk to them about Lana."

"Really?"

"Yeah. While she had me in that box, she got knocked around pretty good by the guy she was with. He said something to her like, 'You're going to pay for that,' and she answered, saying that she had been paying for it all her life."

Jessica looked at the bruise on her arm from her struggle with Lana over the gun. "I could see her look of *good riddance* when that gun went off and she killed the guy.

"When I had her down on the floor, trying to keep her from detonating her suicide belt, she was pleading with me to make a deal with her. It was weird, now that I think about it, because she went right from suicide to wanting a chance at life in America.

"Agent Barry, the agent who is interviewing her at the barn, called me this morning to tell me about her life. She was one of close to a million orphans fleeing Iraq who are trying to find a place to fit in. It makes sense why ISIL has so many young kids joining when you realize they have no other opportunities.

"And the girls! They have nothing. If they *did* keep their family and had an opportunity for a better life, they are still controlled by what their fathers or husbands will allow them to do."

Liam nodded and kept his eyes on the game.

"And that Sharia Law is scary shit! They basically think anyone and everyone who is non-Muslim should be put to death. Women have no rights. They are treated like property, to be abused as men see fit. I just wonder what women's lib would do for those countries. If women had actual rights and opportunities, everyone would respect each other more. Women wouldn't be receiving beatings from the men as a way of life, and children wouldn't see that as their example."

Jessica looked up at Liam. "Are you listening to me?"

"Yeah."

"What did I say?"

"You said Sharia Law was scary shit and how life would be better if women were ruling those countries."

"I'm not saying they have to rule. But they need rights. There is so much hate, judgment, and violence over there. How can they call that a religion?"

Jessica let out a heavy sigh and formulated a speech for the high school students in her head. She was anxious to speak to them. "Maybe Lana's story will inspire an appreciation of their rights and opportunities that many people will never have. They need to appreciate their education and use it to create better opportunities."

Liam tilted his head and raised his brows. "Is this a sermon or a career speech?"

She rolled over and climbed out of bed. "Okay. I get your point."

Liam grabbed her arm. "Hey, where are you going?"

"I want to write some of this down while I'm thinking about it."

Liam gave her his Prince Charming smile. "You can do that later, I thought you came over to make me feel better."

Jessica tilted her head at him and recognized the hungry look in his eyes. She shut off the game with the remote and climbed back in bed, straddling his hips. "Tell me where it hurts, and I'll kiss it and make it all better."

Liam pointed at his lips.

Jessica bent down and kissed him on the lips, tugging his bottom lip gently between her teeth as she pulled away.

He then pointed at his neck.

She sucked on his earlobe and kissed his neck as Liam slid his good hand up her shirt, snapping open her bra.

Jessica sat back, and Liam struggled to unbutton her shirt with his one good hand.

He looked up at her with a slow grin. "It would make me feel better if you took off your clothes."

Jessica pulled off her shirt and grinned down at Liam. "Do you feel better now?"

Liam raised his brows and nodded. "I'm starting to."

Chapter 36
Rondie's friend

Saturday, May 21st, 9:30 a.m.

A few weeks later, Bill was drinking coffee out by the pool with Karen while Emma was inside getting ready to go to work. "Did you see the for sale sign in Peggy's yard?"

Karen sighed. "Yes. I've tried to text her and call her, but she won't have anything to do with me."

"They're living under a cloud of constant suspicion and scrutiny. I don't blame them."

Karen took a sip of her coffee. "What's going to happen to Cal?"

"His story has checked out. He should be cleared of everything, as long as he stays away from that girl. I hear he asked if he could talk to her. His lawyer advised him against it, but now that'll be noted on the record. He needs to get over *her*."

"That was his first real girlfriend."

Bill's phone interrupted their conversation. "Hello?"

Karen assumed his call was business and went inside to warm her coffee.

Bill joined her a few minutes later. "Do you want to go shopping at Queenstown Outlet Stores?"

Karen's brows rose. "Do *you*?"

"No, but my boat is done, and I need a ride over to the Eastern Shore to pick it up. If you could run me over there, I could bring it back to the marina, and we could meet there later for dinner."

Karen's first instinct was to call Peggy to see if she wanted to go shopping, but then remembered Peggy wasn't speaking to her.

"Give me forty-five minutes, and I'll run you over there."

An hour and a half later, Karen dropped Bill at the Kentmoor Marina. "Do you want me to stick around to make sure everything is okay?"

"No, you go on. I've got my phone. I'll call if I need you. Otherwise, I'll see you back at our slip for dinner."

Karen slowed down as she passed the ditch where she and Liam had run off the embankment. Someone had towed the car and left deep ruts along the road. She wondered how Liam was getting along.

Two and a half hours later, Bill pulled into his slip next to Rondie. She had just hopped off her boat and was hugging a friend goodbye.

When Rondie saw his boat, she cupped her hands around her mouth and shouted, "Bill! Can I help you with your lines?"

The sun was in his eyes, so he had trouble seeing Rondie's friend, whose face was concealed under the broad rim of a fishing hat.

Bill tossed her the first line. "That would be great." He pointed to the dock. "Can you tie it on to that cleat?"

He tossed the other line to her friend. He seemed very familiar, but Bill still couldn't see his face. "Thanks, man. Can you tie it to the cleat by the electrical box?"

When Bill finished setting lines and shutting down the engines, he climbed down to join Rondie and her friend on the dock.

Bill pushed his hat back on his head. "Thanks for the help."

"Not a problem. I'm glad to see everything is fixed and running smoothly. It was a beautiful day to be on the water." Rondie hesitated and glanced up at her friend. "You know Director Lowe."

Bill suppressed a laugh. Finally, he understood how she could slip away from crime scenes after shooting someone without leaving footprints, and how she gathered detailed information so quickly.

He extended his hand to meet the Director. "Of course, how are you?"

The Director had a strong, firm handshake. "You did a hell of a job on that information breach."

"Thank you, sir. It should never have happened. But we were able to gain useful information we will be able to use going forward."

"It was great teamwork. I'm sorry for the losses, but there could have been many more."

Bill pressed his lips together and nodded.

The Director shaded his eyes and looked up at the bridge of Bill's boat. "Nice trawler. How many feet?"

"Forty. She's a bit of a mess right now, but you are welcome to come aboard."

The Director extended his hand. "Thank you. Maybe another time. I really have to be leaving. Again, good work."

Bill gave him a parting handshake. "Thank you." He climbed back onto his boat and was snapping canvas over the dashboard up on the fly bridge when he heard someone call his name. He looked down and saw Rondie on the deck of her boat.

Rondie shaded her eyes and called up to Bill. "Join me for a drink?"

"Give me a minute; I'll be right there." He called Karen to touch base.

"Hey Karen, I'm back. Where are you?"

"I'm almost to the marina."

"Oh good. Meet me on Rondie's boat. I'm going to have a drink with her."

Bill ended the call and jumped down to the pier. When he boarded her deck, Rondie was sitting under the shade of the dodger.

She reached into the cooler of ice. "Beer?"

"Sounds great. So, how are you?"

"I'm fine. We just got back from sailing around the Bay. Beautiful day."

Bill raised his beer and smiled. "Nice to know I have friends who know people in high places."

"Yeah, about that. We like to keep our relationship on the QT."

Bill nodded and took a long pull from his beer, remembering Jessica said the same thing. "Not a problem."

Rondie watched Bill lower his eyes. "Don't get the wrong impression. This isn't that kind of relationship."

Rondie picked at the label on her beer. "There are several of us who have officially retired but are still keeping our skills sharp."

Bill's eyebrows shot up. "Really? How does that work?"

"Well, I take my thirty years of sharpshooting and being a lead investigator, trainer, plus my all-around FBI expertise, and add a head of grey hair as a disguise. The wrong people automatically dismiss me as an old white lady, and it gives me an advantage; I can kick the crap out of them before they know what happened, and then I gracefully fade into the wallpaper without anyone giving me a second glance. There are a half dozen of us scattered between here and New York. We are the *Silver Ops*. Sharp-shooting Intelligence Leaders and Vets in the Expert Reserve."

"All women?"

Rondie nodded. "Yep."

Bill digested the information, already thinking of plenty of situations where she could be used to gather information. "Why did you retire?"

"I was sick of working with people who had half my experience and whose opinions I didn't agree with. It was hard for me not to slap their patronizing smirks off their pudgy little cheeks when they had to train me on the newest technology. I wanted to scream at them that I was fighting a war on the other side of the earth, using skills when I was their age that they will never acquire. They are so smug, because they are versed on the newest technology, just because they grew up with their fingers and noses attached to a computer game."

Bill threw his head back and laughed. "I know just how you feel."

Karen walked down the finger dock and rested her hands on the rail. "And how do you know how she feels?"

"Karen! Come aboard. Beer?"

Karen joined them on the deck and shrugged off the bag she was carrying. "No, thanks." She pulled a wine bottle from her bag. "Do you have a corkscrew or puller?"

Rondie lifted the string attached to the handle on the cooler. "Right here."

Bill opened the bottle while Rondie went down to the cabin for a wine glass.

Karen poured a full glass of wine. "What shall we toast to?"

"Teamwork? Success?" suggested Rondie.

"How 'bout peace?" asked Karen.

Bill raised his beer. "Here is to all the incredible women in my life."

They raised their glasses in unison and said, "I'll drink to that!"

The End

Thank you for reading my book!

If you have enjoyed my book, please consider writing a review at amazon.com.

52611276R00106

Made in the USA
Lexington, KY
04 June 2016